JF YA   05-461
MIL

Miller, Deanna

Sky bounce.

DATE DUE

SALEM COUNTY LIBRARY COMMISSION
900 Route 45
Building 3
Pilesgrove, NJ 08098

05-461
D. MILLER
(FIVE OWLS)
4/05
$5.99

An original publication by

Deanna Miller

Publisher's mailing address is listed at
http://www.deannamiller.com.

Copyright © 1995, 2001, 2003 by Deanna Miller

This is a work of fiction. Characters, names, places, and incidents are products of the author's imagination or are used fictitiously. Any resemblance to actual persons, places, or events, past or present, is coincidental.

All rights reserved. No part of this publication may be reproduced, stored in a retrieval system, or transmitted in any form or by any means, electronic, mechanical, recording or otherwise, without permission of the publisher.

ISBN 0-9725424-1-8

Cover illustration © 2003 by Janet J. E. Chui,
http://www.deadfaeries.com

Cover design by Ellipse Design and Deanna Miller

Printed in the U.S.A.

May 2003

I thank the following editors for their helpful advice and their faith in my book: Louisa Dalton, Jean E. Karl, Rob Lentz, John and Marjorie McCall, Frank McGuire, and, most of all, Lavinia N. Miller.

CONTENTS

Part III: The Barren Plane

PART I

The Alula Plane

1

Tristan the Boytaur

Sometimes, when the sweet night air is gentle and quiet enough, I can hear the voices. Slowly they speak, their hushed whispers arising softly from nowhere, drifting back and forth, in and out of nothingness. Though I cannot understand what they say, I feel a strange sadness whenever I listen, for the voices are like the last pleas for hope sent by hopeless souls.

I have told no one about the voices—except, of course, my best friend Tristan, the glowing Boytaur. Tristan hears them, though it seems that no one else does. We both agree it would be better if I never told the others of my kind about the voices: they might shun me like the others of his kind do him just because he glows.

I feel sorry for Tristan because he's an outcast and because he glows. I really do not know how he manages to survive all alone.

I know I never could. At fifteen, I'm still very young—one of the younger Alulas, the winged women who soar through the skies and make the skymounts their homes. As we Alulas are not allowed to go near the land below, where the Mantaurs—or, hoofed men—dwell, Tristan and I must meet in secret. I wait until the night comes and hides me in its darkness before I fly down to his cave. There, we don our flying cloaks; I climb upon his reddish-brown, horselike back; and we bounce-fly through the sky, my arms wrapped around his waist so I won't fall off, my broad wings beating fast and sure. We cannot help but smile at our cleverness. For while the Mantaurs struggle to discover a way to fly like the Alulas and the Alulas try to gain a strength and endurance like that of the Mantaurs, we alone have found the most simple, most obvious solution to the problems of both races.

Bounce-flying is much more exciting than ordinary flight. The first time we tried it I was really scared, but now I've grown so used to it that I hardly ever do regular flying unless I'm with a flit of Alulas and I have to. Flying in a flit—amidst a group of Alulas—I tire easily, and I must stop and rest on one of the skymounts after only a short while. But tonight as I fly with Tristan, instead of stopping on the skymounts, we dive straight for the ground, my feet tingling at the thrill of nothing beneath them but the empty tickling wind. My arms I keep around Tristan's waist; my wings I flap with slow grace, coasting on the wind-waves. And down we drop while up my long hair soars, the dark curls blown back and afloat in the breeze. Then just when it seems sure to go on forever—this great falling-flying—suddenly we're touching ground, bouncing. Suddenly Tristan's four hoofed legs are tensing and flexing: forelegs first, cushioning the impact; hind legs next, pushing us off the spongy earth with terrific force. And wings beating, hooves climbing, we fly. Ever upward we fly—higher than any Mantaur could with his wingless body, faster than any Alula could with her two skinny legs.

Sometimes we bounce-fly in silence, working together so easily that I almost forget we're not one being but two very different ones who, after flying, must part. Other times —times like this—we argue so much I nearly forget to beat my wings. We argue over right and wrong, mostly: Tristan always argues that he's right; I always argue that he's wrong.

"Oh, I don't care who's right and who's wrong anymore!" I finally say with a sigh, smiling into the sea-green eyes that glance back at me, amused. Tristan's glow is striking in the darkness of the night: surrounding his face is a kind of greenish color that complements his reddish-brown hair. I think it's beautiful, but strange. Just like Tristan.

"Well," he says as we plunge down for a bounce, "I know I'm right about one thing: I can and *will* learn how to ride the interplane like the Alulas do, and someday I'm going to travel. First to all the planes on this planet, then to all those on other planets."

The wind sifts through my long hair, sending it flapping out behind me like a third wing—a wing not of pale brown feathers but of dark brown curls. I roll my eyes. Sometimes Tristan can be so exasperating. He knows nothing about the beings of the other planes, or about the aliens on foreign planets, yet he doesn't even worry that they might be hostile. Considering how hostile the others of his own kind are, his unrealistic travel goals don't make sense to me. "Well, I think interplanar travel is dumb," I say. "I wouldn't care if I never did it."

"You're just scared."

I look over Tristan's shoulder and down at the ground, watching it grow closer, closer; listening to the sad voices grow clearer, clearer. "Well, you would be scared, too, if you knew it was something you might *have* to do someday. You're a Boytaur: riding the interplane isn't something you might be ordered to do whether you like it or not."

"Hesper, I just said I was going to do it, didn't I?"

We hit the springy earth with full force. It gives in just enough to cushion Tristan's legs without stopping them from pushing off with even greater force. We head back out easily, my wings beating faster and my heart speeding its pace as if to keep up with them. I gaze up at the scattered skymounts. In the darkness, they resemble unnaturally black clouds that, the higher we fly and the closer they get, blot out larger and larger patches of stars. But though the skymounts are suspended in the atmosphere like clouds, they are made not of water vapor but of rock and soil held together by the tangled roots of trees. After passing many skymounts, we start to round off.

"*I* don't even know how to ride the inter-plane, and I'm an Alula," I say.

"Only because you don't want to know how." He turns and, for a moment, looks me straight in the face. His eyes are brilliant, penetrating. Nowhere else is his glow quite so strong, so green. "You could do it if you wanted to."

I look away. "Well, I don't," I say matter-of-factly.

"Come on! All we have to do is spy on one of their Sendings." Then, hopefully: "Like the one tomorrow night. If we spied on the Sending, we'd both know how to do it."

"Oh, Tris, not that again! You still don't realize how dangerous that is, do you?"

His breath tickles my ear as he leans back and whispers, "You still don't realize how much fun danger is, do you?"

"No!" I whisper.

We lapse into silence as we sail down again, bounce. On our way up, Tristan continues, "Hesper, if you hide from danger, it'll come looking for you anyway. Might as well find it before it finds you." He says it jokingly, but I know he's really serious.

I hate it when he's really serious. "Wise

words from a fifteen-year-old Boytaur!" I say, laughing nervously.

"Come on, Hess," he pleads. "Just this one time."

"What about your glow? It would give us away for sure."

"Not if we're careful. Besides, I don't think the other Alulas see my glow the way you do. They wouldn't even notice. Come on! Aren't you at least a little curious?"

I stare past Tristan and out into the dark night sky. Curious? Of course I am. Curious to know why, for all my life—though I'm told the tradition is a recent one—the Council of the Alulas has been Sending one young Alula after another to an unknown plane to carry out unknown "duties." Curious to know why they have never come back, those Sent Alulas. Even the ones who promised they would, glancing back at me through teary eyes, smiling uncertain smiles.

Yes, I am curious to know. And terrified at the thought of actually finding out.

Tristan's voice grows more serious, more tempting. "If you knew what the Sendings were like, you might not be so afraid if the time came for you to be Sent."

The muscles of my legs tense; the nerves in the bottoms of my feet prickle. I do not want to think about the possibility of being Sent, do not want to face it or acknowledge it, though I can feel it towering above me like a skymount that seems as remote as the moon but can be reached by wing in no time.

"Come on, Hess."

I hesitate. "Well, maybe . . . maybe I will think about it."

With a triumphant shout, Tristan swings his arms back and hugs me.

"Stop it!" I yell. "We could lose balance." But I cannot help smiling.

He does it again, just to tease me. I have to keep my arms around his waist, so I use my elbows to knock his arms away before we head down for another bounce. "Now remember," I say into the cool wind-wave we create, "I said I would just think about it."

"Why don't you give your brain a rest," he says, "and do something for once *without* thinking about it?"

"What's wrong with thinking before acting? It sure wouldn't hurt for you to try it!"

"Hesper, some things aren't meant to be thought about. Take . . . breathing. Do we have to think about breathing? No!"

I laugh. "Luckily for you, too. You'd die of suffocation before you would think to breathe."

"Oh, yeah? Well, you'd be so busy thinking about it that you'd die before you decided to do it."

"Oh, yeah? Oh, *yeah?*" I say, tickling him under his forelegs with my toes.

"Stop it," he mimics. "We could lose balance!" He flails his arms around like a baby Alula learning to fly.

I laugh and tickle him some more.

"Help!" Laughing along, he flounders, then starts kicking his four legs around with the same craziness. I feel my seat wobble beneath me and realize the ground is growing closer—dangerously closer.

My mirth gives way to a panicked, "Enough!" But he's having too much fun to listen: his legs, instead of bracing for the bounce, continue their crazy dance. "We're going to crash!" I say. "Stop it!"

He keeps up the joke until practically the moment before impact, when his legs snap into position with instinctive ease, safely breaking our fall. I stop flapping my wings to prevent him from pushing off again, so we bounce-gallop a few paces and slow to a halt. I shove him hard before sliding off.

"What do you think you were doing?" I shout, planting my hands on my hips and pressing my toes into the cool, mossy ground. "What were you trying to do? Break your legs or break my neck?"

He brushes a few strands of hair away from his face and blinks back at me, still catching his breath. The look I see in his eyes is so thoughtful that despite my anger, I cannot help feeling struck by it.

Light-bearing. Deep-seeing, those eyes. What is it they search for? What is it they find in the darkness of my own brown eyes?

"It must be scary . . . to be so afraid," he finally says, his voice soft with sympathy. Then just as I'm about to argue, he says, "Come get a snack with me," and turns and gallops off in the direction of his cave. I stand there with the sad voices in my ears and my hands on my hips, fuming.

I sigh. Sometimes Tristan can be so exasperating.

2

Fear Not

I think of Tristan's words as I fly back up to my home skymount and sneak back into my bed. There, I dream that I'm chosen to be Sent. It's a nightmare familiar to every young Alula—even, I think, those lucky few whose blood relation to the Council exempts them from being Sent. But familiar or not, it still makes me sit bolt upright, then lie back with a relieved sigh, when I hear my aunt come in to wake me.

"Goodness!" Aunt Sern says, shaking her head. "I didn't mean to scare you." For a moment I think I see sympathy in her eyes, but then I blink away the haze, and her face sharpens into its usual picture of detachment. Although Aunt Sern has taken care of me ever since my mother was Sent when I was eight years old, my aunt has never allowed herself to get close to me.

"What time is it?" I ask.

"Time for you to be flitting your little self out of here. Hurry up or you'll be late for the learnings!"

I stretch a nice self-indulgent stretch, raising my wings high above my head and yawning up at the low brown ceiling of my little room. Aunt Sern carefully uses one of her wings to turn up the lamp beside my bed. I let my eyes linger for a moment on the underside of her wing where some skin of her arm still shows through the feathers. Most Alulas are not bothered by the way their arms gradually grow into their wings. It's a natural part of aging. But I dread it because, without separate arms to hold onto Tristan while my wings flap, bounce-flying will be impossible.

"I don't know why it is," continues Aunt Sern, "but you're getting harder and harder to wake up every morning. You certainly get to bed early enough, though."

I smile to myself as I step down onto the feather-woven rug and slip out of my nightdress into my flying cloak. Who wants to sleep when they can bounce-fly? I picture Tristan sleeping in his cave and think how lucky he is to have no one to wake him up and make him go to any learnings. But then I remember tonight's Sending and feel panicked at the thought of the secret meeting I normally look forward to all day. Oh, why does Tristan always want to do such dangerous things?

I flip my learning-sack over my shoulder and head for the door.

"How about something to eat?" Aunt Sern calls after me.

"I'll grab an apple at the surface."

I close the door before she can start her protest, then hurry along the dim tunnelway, keeping my wings folded at my sides so they won't bump the lamps sticking out from the curved tunnel walls. The air smells of roots and soil—not the moist, spongy soil of the ground, but the dry, airy soil of the skies.

What am I going to tell Tristan? I think as I greet an Alula rushing the other way. The Alula's face is familiar, but we nod at each other without smiling, as is customary.

No. I must tell him no, I assure myself, walking up the stairway to the surface of the skymount. With each quick step, the air smells a little fresher and the tree roots grow a little bolder in their push through the cracks of the walls. I leap up the last steps two at a time, knock forward the door to the surface, and climb out into the morning sunlight.

By the time I wash my face in a spring and pick my breakfast off a nearby tree, the learning flit has already gathered and started reciting the Poem of the Planes. For a second I think about skipping the learnings altogether, but the teacher catches sight of me, so I hasten to join the circle, quietly mumbling along:

"Different planes, one fate ties them all.
Should one plane slip, then each shall fall.
Should one break loose and drop away,
Then none shall last another day.
For where one stops, the others end,
And if one curves, the others bend:
Different dimensions of one space,
Different places at the same place."

The teacher turns and walks past several trees to a little creek. As always, we follow in silence, watch her scoop up a bucket full of swiftly darting water with her wing and set it down before us.

"Observe the waters of the creek," she says. Her words are a familiar repetition. "From one angle it is like this." She gestures at the sparkling water in the bucket, where a few little fish swim around in smooth circles. "Home to the most conscious of the water creatures: those with the most developed brains." She holds a round magnifying scope over the water and says, "From another angle it looks like this." The clear surface transforms into a swarm of smaller creatures that wriggle around rather aimlessly. "Home to creatures who are less conscious, who have less developed brains."

She turns the dial on the magnifying scope until the surface changes again to show even tinier creatures: single-celled ones with whip-like tails and fine little hairs all around their oval bodies. Their jerky movements seem to be completely random, without purpose. "And from another angle it is like this. Home to the least conscious creatures: those with the most primitive brains."

After we have seen it, she dumps the water back into the creek and scans us with eyes like my aunt's, only colder, prouder. "The same water is different from different angles. Looking at the creek now, we cannot see the different levels we saw with the magnifying scope. But they are still there—there and not there. There because we know they are; not there because we cannot see they are. They are at different levels of existence. Different places at the same place." She pauses, looks us over. When I feel her eyes settle on me, I try to act alert, like I'm hearing this for the first time instead of the thousandth. She continues, "It is mental awareness that separates the creatures of the creek. But what is it that separates the creatures of the planes?"

"Awareness of the Great Alula," we chime.

"Yes," she says. "To understand the parallel planes, think of the levels of the creek."

I feel keenly the sleep I've missed by the time we start the recitation of the Holy Tablets. Today my teacher chooses the chapter called "Birth of the Planes." As she points to the Alula next to me and my classmate begins the recitation, I battle my drowsiness and nervously go over the words in my mind.

My classmate's voice comes through an anxious mist. "The Great Alula reached out to our planet and spun it with the tip of Her gentle wing. And She said, 'This planet I divide into different planes of existence.' "

The teacher points to another Alula, then another, and so on:

" 'And I fill these planes with creatures

parallel, but separated from one another by their different distances from Me.' "

" 'On the first plane I place the farthest away: those who neither know Me nor ever speak My name.' "

" 'On the second plane I place those who know of Me but cannot feel Me.' "

" 'On the third plane I place two races: one of the sky who can feel Me and one of the ground who cannot.' "

" 'On the fourth plane I place those who can feel Me at any moment, but only if they so choose.' "

The teacher points to me next, and I wake up fast. As confidently as I can, I say, " 'The fifth plane I leave barren. No life of this planet do I place there, but all those who pass through it may never again deny their link to Me.' "

She points to someone else again, and I breathe a sigh of relief as that classmate recites the part about the planes closest to the Great Alula. Eventually the teacher nods in approval and tells us to form a circle for the practice Sending.

"Close your eyes," she says, "and imagine you are being Sent. Take your fears and let them go. Relax. Put all your trust in the Great Alula. Know that She loves you despite your fears, and give your whole self to Her care. Let go, and feel Her power."

As usual, I have trouble letting go of my fears. But I remind myself of the teacher's words: "Know that She loves you despite your fears." And I can let go just enough to feel a lightness rise up within me, then tingle through me like a soft breeze blowing from the inside.

My teacher's voice jars me out of my peaceful state. "Good. You are dismissed for lunch and free-flying."

We eat lunch and start our free-flying all in one large flit. But as soon as we know the teacher has stopped watching us, we start separating. Some break away in groups of two or three, but most of us fly off on our own. Most of us know better than to get close to those who, sooner or later, could only be Sent away from us. I fly by myself over the sky-mounts, worrying about tonight's Sending and gazing down at the grown-ups as they carry out their daily tasks. Many are out of view because they are inside the skymounts at their places of work. But I see some tending to their gardens, gathering fruit and nuts from the woods, and caring for the Alulas still too young to go to the learnings.

The most interesting sight, though, is a group of Alulas kneeling down at the edge of a clearing, communicating by sound and gesture with a group of animals. For a couple of years now the grown-ups have been negotiating with the animals for permission to move our homes to the surfaces of the skymounts instead of their insides. So far, the animals have not been very cooperative, and who can blame them? If we Alulas moved to the surfaces, the animals would lose quite a big chunk of living space.

I alight at the opposite edge of the clearing, hoping for a better view of the negotiations. As I move to hide behind the thick trunk of a tree, I hear someone whisper, "Hesper!" And looking around, I jump at the sight of two faces peering out at me from behind another tree trunk.

"What are you two doing?" I ask Jana and Layn, members of my learning flit, as they exchange a meaningful glance and giggle.

"Same thing you're doing," says Jana. She opens her mocking eyes wide. "Spying."

"Oh." I spread my wings to take off. "Well, have fun."

"What's the matter, Hesper?" asks Layn, the mockery spreading from Jana's face to hers. "Afraid you could get caught? Afraid you could get in trouble . . . for once in your life?"

"Afraid," Jana chimes in, "we'll shatter your safe image—get you Sent—by telling everyone we saw you do something *daring?"*

I feel my face turning red. *They don't know how I sneak out at night,* I tell myself. *How I bounce-fly with a forbidden friend, press my toes into forbidden ground. . . .*

But I cannot fool myself. I know very well that any other Alula would do the same if she met Tristan. Any Alula who met him would want to sneak out to meet him, whether she was daring or not. I let my wings fall. My heart starts swelling with shame. What brings me out every night is not my own bravery, but Tristan's charm.

"Come on, Jana," says Layn. "We must get closer to the action. Only a chicken wing would hide this far back."

I do not look at them as they leave. I'm too busy looking in at myself—as they see me, as

Tristan sees me, as I see me. Most of all, as I see me.

My mother's voice plays in my memory, quoting the words of the Holy Tablets the way she often would:

"Fear not. For what you fear is what you will attract."

The swelling in my heart overflows into my eyes, and I choke back a bitter sob. For a moment all I want to do is see my mother again—to undo her Sending and have her standing right here with me. But when I think of those sympathetic eyes I can never again see and those comforting curls I can never again bury my face in, the shame curdles into anger. Steady anger that stays with me for the rest of the day—through the last hours of the learnings, dinner with my aunt, bedtime—until the dark night finally comes and hides me as I fly down to Tristan's cave.

"Oh, all right!" I say over Tristan's shoulder before we've even bounced our second bounce. "Let's get it over with!"

Tristan shoots me a look halfway between shock and glee. "What? You mean the Sending?"

I nod, smiling nervously at the funny expression of amazement on his face.

"But I haven't even started bugging you about it yet!"

"Well, too late now. I've already decided."

He laughs as he faces forward again. "That's what I like about you, Hess. You're just like the animals of the skymounts."

"How do you mean?" I ask.

"Well, that night you took me to see the animals, they ran away at first. Remember? But we waited quietly, and after a while they came out." He turns to me, thoughtful, no longer smiling. "And to me that was more exciting than if they'd run up to us first thing."

I look away. I can feel myself beaming and my cheeks growing warm despite the cool breeze. "Well, we really should hurry. . . ."

"Okay, let's go!" he shouts happily as we head down for another bounce.

"Give it a good bounce, now!" I say, holding on tight. "The Sendings are held way up on the High Skymount!"

"Don't worry; I will!"

The dread comes back as a physical ache, but the night air feels good whipping against my face and wings. Below us, the voices cry out: vague at first, then a little louder, singing their lament.

I close my eyes, let Tristan guide for a while. Try to relax. Feel the voices fade in and out: rise, then fall; rise, then fall.

I wish we could glide down forever and never have to bounce back up.

3

The Sending

"Are we almost there?" Tristan asks impatiently.

"Just a little higher," I say, gazing up into the star-flecked sky.

"But we've passed just about all the skymounts . . . and I'm tired."

"Oh, stop complaining," I tease. "You're the one who wanted to go so badly, remember?"

We fly in silence. Soon the dark, shapeless outline of the High Skymount beckons from above like a beautiful temptation best resisted.

"I'm scared," I say in a small voice.

"I know."

"Tris, let's go back."

"Too late for that," he whispers, entranced.

We overshoot the High Skymount, then begin our descent, aiming for the woods along its edge so we won't be seen by the Alulas in the wide clearing at its center. I feel my hands shaking as I glimpse them on our way down. Gathered in one giant circle is the entire royalty of the skymounts—from the old Council members, who have no arms at all, to the youngest members of their family flits, who have whole arms just like mine. They all look so proud and fearless as they stand there in silence, their eyes closed and their elegant Sending dresses fluttering in the breeze like pairs of rebellious wings. My heart pounds with renewed anger. Of course they're fearless. They Send others; they need not worry about being Sent themselves.

We slam-hit the surface as silently as we can. Landing on the skymounts is much more jarring than landing on the ground below.

"Get your hair out of my face, will you?" Tristan whispers, waving away the mass of curly tangles.

I flip my hair back. Tristan hates landing on the skymounts because my hair always falls forward into his face. Usually I find it funny, but nothing is funny to me now. Not with the Council so close.

"That reminds me . . . here," Tristan says, pulling something out of the pocket of his flying cloak. "I carved this out of that skymount wood you gave me." He hands me what looks like a misshapen comb, and my fingers confirm a row of uneven but smooth teeth.

The pleasure of surprise makes me forget about the Sending for a moment. I wonder how long it took Tristan to carve out all those teeth, and I smile, hoping it took him quite a while. "I love it. Thank you, Tris." I start the comb through my hair, and we both struggle to hold back our laughter when it gets stuck there.

"I wish we were allowed to be friends," he says.

"It's not our fault we Alulas aren't allowed to come near the Mantaurs," I point out. "They endanger our lives."

It's true, too: even the necessity of the Merging is a dangerous task. I've never been old enough to take part in the Merging, but I remember my family flit warning me how risky it is. The Mantaurs, interested only in fighting the Alulas, view the Merging as just another opportunity to tear off some Alulas' wings. So the Alulas must spray entire packs of Mantaurs from overhead with a strong herb to make the Mantaurs drowsy first. Then they have to do quickly the thing necessary to perpetuate our kind, and leave before the Mantaurs' drowsiness wears off and they can attack.

Tristan looks in the direction of the gathering, now masked by the trees. "It puffs the Alulas up—comparing themselves to the Mantaurs—doesn't it? Makes them feel holy when they're really not." I'm about to argue when he abruptly straightens and says, "I'm moving in closer."

"No, wait! They could see us."

"Hess, their eyes are closed." He inches forward.

"Wait! If they see me—especially with you, a Boytaur—"

"It's okay." He reaches behind, takes my hands in his, and holds them there, steadying them. "It'll be okay." He creeps to the edge of the woods and peeks out at the clearing.

I want to leave. I want to jump right off him and fly far away. But as I watch the back of his head as he strains forward in the darkness, all I can think of is that first time we ever hid out together. And I know I cannot desert him.

The first time we hid out was also the first time we met. I had been flying longer than I

should have on that memorable day, and a
sharp cramp in my wing had sent me plunging
straight down to the forbidden ground. Never
before had my feet touched anything but the
dry soil of the skies, and the strange feel of the
moist, springy ground made the bottoms of my
bare feet prickle with fear. No sooner had I
begun surveying that treeless, hilly land for a
place to hide when a faint rumbling sound
filled my ears.

Not knowing if I was hearing a herd of
animals or a hunting pack of Mantaurs, I
froze, thinking of all the terrible stories I'd
heard about the Mantaurs. How they viciously
devoured the animals of the ground and even
turned on their own kind, killing each other
for food when there were fruit and nut bushes
all around them. (The Mantaurs have no
qualms when it comes to what they eat; they
even chew on the evil weeds that the Great
Alula forbids.) My common sense returned to
me then, and I ran into the nearest of many
hillside caves. The inside of the cave was just
as smooth as its sloping exterior: I frantically
searched for rocks to hide behind but found
only a curtain of mossy vines growing up the
back wall. I squeezed between the vines and

the wall, gritting my teeth at the shock of the dank, clammy sandwich. But the physical discomfort didn't distract me for long, because I heard another sound—a very nearby sound— and saw a Boytaur slip into the cave after me. I froze again. I felt he knew I was there, though he did not look at me. He pressed his horse's body against the side of the cave and strained his head forward, peering out in the direction of the rumbling. I had enough time to notice that he was about my age and that he had a curious glow about him before I saw the other Mantaurs and Boytaurs.

They were galloping so fast that at first I was relieved to think they were passing right by. But they circled back and spread out, slowing to a halt all around the cave. I nearly stopped breathing at the sound of their hooves on the hilltop above me and the sight of several large, muscular forms just outside the cave's mouth.

Then I heard them speak, and I sucked in my breath in horror.

"I'll tear her wings off!" growled one.

"No, whoever finds her does!" yelled another. "Then we'll all take turns torturing her."

I pressed harder against the soft wall, pray-

ing to the Great Alula to let me sink right into
it, disappear. The thought of the Mantaurs attacking each other and the animals of the
ground had always made me ill. But that was
nothing compared with the sick panic that
throbbed in my head at the thought of them
attacking *me*.

I was still desperately praying when one
of the Mantaurs headed straight for the cave
opening.

I dug my fingernails so deep into the
cave's wall that it hurt. But before the Mantaur came close enough to see inside, the
glowing Boytaur stepped out from his hiding
place, blocking the way. The Mantaur stared
at the Boytaur, his eyes wild.

"Go back where you came from, glowing
freak!" the Mantaur shouted. He spat out a
wad of evil weed he had been chewing. It
barely missed the Boytaur.

I dug my nails deeper into the wall.

"No," said the Boytaur with defiant confidence. *"You* go back."

The Mantaur glared at him, open hatred
boiling in those wild eyes. Yet there was fear
in his eyes, too, and to my disbelief he backed
away from the cave without even looking in-

side. The rest of the Mantaurs followed his
lead: soon the whole pack had gone off somewhere else to hunt for me, shouting back and
forth about my location.

I let out a sigh.

Cautiously, the Boytaur turned and can-
tered on his hoofed legs to where I stood, still
plastered against the wall. "If you come with
me to my cave, you'll be safe from them," he
said shyly.

I studied his face, wary of any Mantaur.
And it was then that I noticed his eyes were
the center of his light, the sun that gave off his
wondrous rays. . . .

The sound of Tristan's eager whisper jerks
me back to the frightening present. "Come on,
Hess!" he urges, giving my hands a squeeze.
"Take a look at this."

I lean forward on his back and peer over
his shoulder. One Alula has broken from the
ring of faces and, eyes still closed, has begun
walking quietly forward. She is no older than I
am and, from the expression on her face, not
much braver either. I recognize her at once.
Often I have flown in the same flit with her,
but never have I tried talking to her or re-

sponded with much friendliness when she tried talking to me. I'm glad of it now, too. Glad she won't be yet another Alula for me to miss.

Tristan whispers. "Is she—"

"Shhh. Yes," I say. "She is the one they're Send—"

"Shhh! Look."

As the Alula takes her place at its center, the circle closes up, and another Alula—one of the Council members—spreads her wings and lifts her wrinkled face toward the treetops swaying beyond her shut eyelids. The other Alulas raise their heads as she speaks:

"Great Alula, Goddess of the Winged Women, please take this child safely to the plane of our choosing: the human plane—an existence parallel to ours, at once here and not here. Please guide her to fulfill her duty there. We sacrifice her for the good of all the planes, and our blessing goes with her." She pauses, then cries, "Great Alula, we give her to You!"

I shiver. There is a visible relaxing in the circle, then a flurry of wings—wings that fly up and down as if moved by another force, like leaves dancing on windblown boughs. I can still feel Tristan's hands in mine, and I hold them tight. When the beating finally stops and the circle starts to break up, the Alula in the center is gone.

"Wow," Tristan breathes.

"All right, it's over. Time to go," I say, spreading my wings anxiously.

"I wonder why they Sent her to the human plane," he ponders, ignoring my words.

"Come on, let's get out of here."

"I wonder how it felt for her," he says.

"Well, it felt pretty unpleasant for me, so can we just—"

"Okay, okay."

The Alulas are walking away now, heading for the nearest entrance to the High Skymount's interior. They look content, at peace. But it's a cold content, a proud peace. Tristan lets out a final wistful sigh, and we briefly gallop as best we can between the trees, then lift off. We're just about to clear the skymount's edge and dive down into the black sky when I feel uneasy and glance back over my shoulder.

My uneasiness is not calmed by the sight of a young Alula, face upturned and eyes open wide, staring right up at me.

4

Parting

"They're going to Send me."

I'm standing at the mouth of Tristan's cave, talking to the glow beyond the darkness inside.

"They're going to Send me," I repeat, this time in a loud voice that quivers from crying.

Tristan practically gallops to the entrance. "What?" His face is frantic as he takes my hand and pulls me inside. "Why?"

"Because they saw me."

"What!"

"Because of that Alula I told you about—the one I saw watching us as we were leaving. She recognized me, the feather-fanning tattle-tale! I just finished meeting with the Council."

He stares at me, unbelieving. "You mean that . . . ?"

"Yes." I sniffle, wiping my eyes. "They've called an emergency Sending. They're going to Send me later tonight."

"Tonight! But they just had a Sending last night! They can't—" He stops and looks at me sadly, as if he's just noticed my tears. His next words are quiet. "It's my fault, Hess."

"No," I say and laugh a little, though it really isn't funny at all. Tristan pulls me forward and puts his arms around me. Somehow hugging him makes me feel sorry for myself all over again, and I cry even more.

"You can't go riding the interplane without me," he says gently. "You have to wait until I figure out how to do it, too."

I pull away. "Sure. I can just say, 'Hey, you know that Boytaur you caught me with at your Sending? Well, he wants to go with me, so you can't Send me until he's ready.' "

"Why can't you hide from them? Hide here with me!"

"They would find me," I say hopelessly. "They know all about you now."

"Hess, you can't go." His voice is pleading. "You're not ready."

I shake my head. How many times have I said those words to an Alula before her Sending? How strange to hear them said to me now! To be the one Sent, not the one left behind. "They think I am ready. They say . . .

they say I must carry out a great duty for the parallel planes."

"What duty?" Tristan sits down to listen, his four legs folding underneath his horselike trunk.

I sigh. It was hard for me to digest the reason for the Sendings, and it would be hard to talk about it. "The parallel planes have gotten off balance. So the Council has been Sending young Alulas to live on the human plane to restore the balance."

Tristan frowns. "How does that restore the balance?"

"Well, the Council members say there are aliens living, concealed, among the humans."

I pause, remembering. Seeing, again, those wrinkled old faces as they leaned in around me, their eyes little stabs of brightness in the dim room. "The balance of the planes is off: this we feel," they said. "And there is an alien intrusion: this, too, we feel. It disturbs us. It smothers us, pressing down on our world. . . ." But all I felt pressing down on me then was the weight of their watchful eyes. And as they talked on about the evil aliens and their effect on the planes, I looked away—up at the wall behind them—focusing on a shapeless stain that clung there like a patch of rotted moss. . . .

I shake the memory away with a shiver. "Remember how I told you the planes are like the levels of the creek water?"

"Yes. Each plane's beings have a different awareness of the Great Alula."

"Right. Well, the awareness on the human plane is supposed to be better than ours. But the aliens don't belong there. Their awareness is like the Mantaurs', so they're making the awareness on the human plane too similar to our plane."

Tristan's face turns grave with discovery. "But if the awareness is too similar. . . ."

"Then the planes themselves—physically —become too similar."

"Are you saying the human plane and ours could actually, somehow, blend together?"

I hesitate, not wanting to sound bleak but not wanting to lie either. "Yes, they could blend," I say quietly, "destroying both—and eventually all—the planes."

"Great Alula!" he exclaims. He jumps to his hooves and starts pacing around the cave.

"Don't swear, Tris."

"That could actually happen? Are they

sure? Unless Alulas like you go there to offset the aliens' effect?"

"That's what they say. But the aliens are not just on the human plane. The Council says they're spreading to the barren plane, too."

"What?" His tail swishes involuntarily, like it always does when he's upset. "Nothing grows on the barren plane. How can these aliens survive there?"

"I don't know. But the Council thinks the aliens know how to ride the interplane and are Sending messengers to the other planes, just like we Alulas are." I wring my hands, Tristan's alarm exacerbating my own.

He shakes his head. "This is all very far-fetched. Why can't the Council members Send themselves and find out for sure?"

I shrug. "They run everything on the sky-mounts. Besides, they're too old. They need Alulas to live out their lifetimes on the human plane."

"Live the rest of your life away from your home, on a strange plane, just because they think it'll help the balance?"

Self-pity washes over me like cool mist over aching wings. "They say that because I associate—and fly—with a Boytaur, which is forbidden, and because I spied on one of the Sendings, which is also forbidden, they think I'm perfect for the task. They say they need 'young Alulas who are not crippled by fear.' " I quote the Council's words with sarcasm.

Tristan stops pacing and throws up his hands. *"You?* You're afraid of everything!"

"I know—that's what I tried to tell them! But all they said was, 'Based on your actions, we find that unbelievable.' "

He sighs heavily. "I've gotten you into a great big mess, haven't I?"

"It's not all your fault." I flop down on the cave's soft floor, feeling helpless and drained. Tristan paws the ground, his front right hoof more agitated than ever as it digs its usual circle patterns in the moss.

"You know," I say after some time has passed, "on this plane where they Send me, I'll forget everything I know here."

His hoof freezes in mid-circle.

"That's why they never come back—the Alulas they Send. When the Council Sends an Alula, she loses all memory of the life she leaves."

Tristan looks up in shock but says nothing.

I take one of my long curls and nervously

twist it around my finger. The dread settles in my stomach like a nausea. "Oh, Tris, I'm afraid of forgetting."

He kicks the ground, then says down to it, "I'll miss you, but you won't miss me. No fair." He forces a smile, but it collapses into the most dejected look I've ever seen on him.

That look makes me want to cry all over again. I decide I'd better leave before I do just that. "Well, I should go," I say reluctantly. But I take my time getting to my feet.

"No—wait! Let's at least bounce-fly one last time."

The desperation in his voice sets off a terrible ache in me, and I blink several times to hold the feeling down. "Tris, I have to get back before the Sending. They could be looking for me." I turn, step slowly toward the mouth of the cave.

"Hess, wait!"

I swing back around and meet his eyes. Eyes like lights that reach up from somewhere deep inside him and shine straight into my feelings, into a place way down that I scarcely know. I do not want to forget those eyes.

"I wish . . . I mean. . . ." he falters, suddenly awkward. "Don't forget to comb that mess before the ceremony," he finally says, gesturing at my hair.

My hands fly to my hips; my wings expand in mock indignation. But I cannot help laughing when he laughs.

"I swear, you are the most exasperating Boytaur I know!"

"Not to mention the *only* Boytaur," he teases. Then, his laughter converted to a shaky hope, he comes over and takes my hands in his. "Oh, Hess, don't be afraid. You'll be all right." His voice, though tender, does not soothe me; it just reminds me that I may never hear him speak again. "And we *will* see each other someday—I promise. If not on this plane, then another."

"Yes: another," I say and smile cheerfully for Tristan's sake.

My smile fades as soon as I take off for the skymounts. I'm very worried for the planes, but the heaviness of that problem is still too new and unreal to me, too impossibly awful to be true. So thoughts of my duty to the planes, my murky future, are all overshadowed by a sense of loss I haven't felt since my mother was Sent. I should have been more careful. I should have kept my distance from Tristan, just as I did the Alulas. What was I thinking? Now I feel angry and lonely, knowing that if we ever do meet again, I won't even know him. Tristan is just as vital to my life as his powerful legs are to bounce-flying. Without him, who will I argue with? How will I bounce-fly? And without me, how will poor Tris fly at all?

Please, Great Alula, Goddess of the Winged Women, please, *please* do not let me forget about my dear friend Tristan, the glowing Boytaur. Or the wonderful feel of cool wind against my wings. Or the strange sadness of the voices from nowhere. . . .

Please.

PART II

The Human Plane

5

The New Boy in School

Sometimes, if I'm all alone and I get really quiet, I can hear this voice.

It's a nice voice, though sort of muffled. I don't know what it says—only that it calls my name. Sometimes I just like to sit and listen to it, wondering who it is, *what* it is, and feeling less lonely knowing it sounds lonely, too. Sometimes the sound of it scares me and I start to think I'm mentally ill, like those people who hear voices and even talk back to them. Sometimes I wish I could shut it up— like when I'm trying to study for a test, which is fairly often now that I'm a junior in high school.

Sometimes I think, *What if this life I know is only a dream, and the voice is someone bending over me as I sleep, saying, "Wake up, Hesper!"—calling me back to the real world, where I belong?*

I don't know. Sometimes I think too much.

Even now, as I walk down the crowded hallway of Spring Ridge High School, thinking about thinking too much, I'm thinking too much. My friend Marcie thinks too much, too. She's walking right next to me, her books smashed against her side in a tight armlock—as if anyone would actually want to swipe something like *Our World of Chemistry*. The problem with Marcie is she does most of her thinking out loud.

"Hesper, I tell you—you've got to see him! He's sooo cute. That's it—I have to meet this guy! If only he weren't so shy, though. How can I bring him out? Let's see . . . I could bump into him and drop my books. No, too typical. Hmm . . . I could ask him where some class is. No, why would *I* ask *him* where a class is? He's the new kid, not me." She turns to me and sighs. "Hesper, help me."

I haven't really been paying much attention to Marcie. I'd rather be alone somewhere, listening for the voice. I don't know why, but I'm worried about it. The last time I heard the voice was over a month ago, and I'm starting to miss it in a way I never thought I would. "Okay," I say, trying to focus on Marcie, "now who's this guy again?"

Marcie rolls her eyes. "Hesper, you aren't listening to a word I say! He's the new boy in the wheelchair. He's sooo cute—Oh, hi, John!—but he seems like one of those loner types. You've got to help me think of a way to meet him."

I sigh. "Okay. Umm, is he in our grade?"

"Yeah, I think so," she says.

"And did you say he's in a wheelchair?"

"Yeah. Anne heard he messed up both legs in a hang gliding accident, and that's why he's temporarily in a wheelchair. Anne said he's a real daredevil. That could be a problem, huh? Do you think maybe he's only interested in wild girls? Or maybe he just assumes girls like me wouldn't want to go hang gliding with him. Or maybe—"

"Okay," I say, laughing. "Why don't you find that out after you meet him?"

"Good idea." Her voice lowers to an eager whisper. "Come on, let's turn down this hall real quick. His locker's this way."

I laugh again. Marcie likes someone new just about every week, but I've got to hand it to her: when she likes a guy, he gets her complete devotion, if only for a week. "Marcie, I've got to go to English. I'm gonna be late."

"Oh, come on! Don't you want to see what he looks like?" she pleads.

"No, I'd rather—"

"Hesper, look out!" Marcie cries, grabbing my arm.

And I do look out. But only in time to glimpse the flash of a wheelchair shooting like a popped cork into my path before I find myself sprawled across the floor watching feet jet past me—and feeling really stupid.

"Get out of the way!" comes a shout from the stampede above.

"Watch out!" says someone else.

Marcie is on her knees in an instant. "Oh, here, let me get these for you," she is saying—but not to me.

Dazed, I start to get up, but as I rise, the strangest thing happens:

I hear the voice. Only this time I'm in the middle of a crowd, hearing it. This time it isn't muffled, but clear and close, practically as close as . . .

As the boy leaning forward in his wheelchair, saying to me, "I'm really sorry. I just didn't see you. Are you okay?"

I can't answer him. I can only stare, awestricken, at this boy sitting before me.

It isn't just his voice, though. It's how he stares back, rapt and waiting, as if he's actually glad he's knocked into me. It's how his green eyes, his face, his very clothes seem to glow from some hidden light. It's how sure I feel that I've seen him, *known* him, somewhere before.

"You're not hurt, are you?" he asks.

Realizing how dumb I must look standing there gaping, I say, "Oh, no, I'm okay," and make a hasty lunge for a fallen history book.

"Are *you* okay?" Marcie asks him, smiling, as she hands him his books.

"Yeah, I'm okay. Thanks a lot," he adds, patting his books and setting them down on his lap.

"No problem," Marcie says with the coy tilt of an eyebrow. "Feel free to crash into *me* next time."

He smiles at her, then turns once more to me. His eyes are like flashlights shining up from the bottoms of green seas.

"Well, sorry again."

I smile shyly. "It's okay."

As he starts to leave, I concentrate on straightening my books, wishing my hands would stop their ridiculous shaking. After all,

I don't want Marcie to think I like him or anything.

"Lucky witch," Marcie whispers in my ear
after he's gone. "I think he did that on purpose!" With that, she turns and sashays to the
stairs.

The whole exchange is over in an instant,
but it's an instant that leaves my heart pounding and my legs trembling as I hurry down the
hallway to my English class.

6

Dream-Flying

English—then chemistry, history, and al-gebra—drift by like clouds in the distance. I spend them all wondering about the boy in the wheelchair. *But why?* I think. *Why?*

Not because of his glow; that I can explain away. I've seen people who glow before. I've told my mom about it, and she said that all people have auras, some stronger than others, and that I must have the ability to see those stronger auras.

But the boy's familiar voice I can't explain away, or the definite feeling I get that I know him. *How do I know him?* I ask myself as I pretend to pay attention to my teachers. *Where have I known him?* I just can't remember.

I don't see him again in the hallway, even though I stay on the lookout for his wheel-chair. By the time the final bell rings, I'm still wracking my brain. *But for what?* I ask myself as I climb the school bus and ride home. *For what?*

It's like grasping for a dream forgotten at the instant of waking. One of those elusive dreams you want so badly to remember, but the harder you try, the faster it fades away. And after all the straining, all the brain-wracking, the only thing you know about the dream is that you dreamt it, nothing more.

It was hard enough before to concentrate on my homework when the voice kept talking to me. Tonight it's even harder to care about atoms and elements, molecules and compounds, knowing that the voice wasn't just a voice, but a real person. A person who looked at me like *he* knew *me*, too.

Marcie calls me at her usual time: dinner hour.

"I've got to eat dinner, Marcie."

"Wait!" she pipes from the other end. "Did you watch the news tonight?"

I scowl. Watching the news, hearing about all the latest horrors people have committed, always grips me with an absurd anger. Absurd because I know there's no way I can foresee the crimes and stop them from happening, but I still feel angry that I can't somehow.

"You know I don't watch the news any-

more, Marcie," I say. "Who needs a daily re-
minder that awful things are happening and
there's nothing you can do about it?"

"But Hesper, you have to know what's going on in the world."

The cheerfulness in her voice brings out
the sarcasm in my own. "Oh, I know what's
going on. People are destroying nature, going
to war, going on shooting sprees—"

"Yeah, but—"

"—instead of hunting animals, people are
hunting people. And it's always open season."

"All right, all right!" she says. "Geez,
Hesper! All I'm saying is tonight's news was
worth watching. There was another one of
those car accidents I told you about—you
know, where people think they see someone in
the road but there's no one there."

"Really? What happened?"

"Some lady ran up on a curb. She said she
was driving along when out of nowhere came
a guy on a horse, and she swerved, but she
was sure she still hit him. Only there *was* no
guy on a horse. Not anywhere around the
scene. But the lady was still hysterical, saying
she'd hit him."

"Wow. Was she drunk or something?"

"No," Marcie says, her voice emphatic. "And here's the weird part: she messed up the underside of her car when she went up on the curb, but there was also a dent on the side of her car. There was no explanation for the dent, other than she *had* hit someone."

I get an odd feeling in my stomach that has nothing to do with hunger. "That sure is weird. It doesn't make any sense." Then, noticing my mom beckoning to me from the kitchen, I say, "Hey, can I call you back later? It's dinner time."

"Well, I probably won't be home later," she says. "Hey, what did you think of that new guy?"

"Oh . . . ummm, he's okay, I guess. I mean—"

"You like him, don't you?" she cuts in, abrupt as ever.

"What?" I exclaim. "Marcie, how could I possibly like him? I don't even . . . know him," I finish weakly.

"I saw the way you two looked at each other today—and his crashing into you was no accident. I think he likes you, too."

"Oh, come on, Marcie!"

"No, it's okay—really. I'm not sure he's

my type after all. You can have him if you want."

"Gee, thanks," I say. "Now let me go eat."

"Okay. See ya tomorrow."

"Bye." I join Mom in the kitchen, helping myself to some vegetables and rice.

"Is Marcie trying to play matchmaker again?" Mom asks, sitting down with her own plate.

"Sort of."

Mom pulls her hair away from her face and clips it. Like mine, her hair is dark brown and curly, but hers is shoulder-length whereas I like mine as long as it'll grow, which at this point means down to my waist. "You look afraid," she says. "Anything wrong?"

I shrug as I take my seat, and she quotes the Bible the way she often does: "I sought the Lord, and He answered me; He delivered me from all my fears."

Sometimes Mom's enthusiasm for the Scriptures can get annoying, but she never quotes the Bible in judgment, only to comfort. And now the words do bring comfort, lifting me beyond the oppressiveness of the TV that lurks in the corner like a troll, dark and silent, nursing its grim secrets.

"Marcie was talking about the news again," I explain. "I've told her before I don't want to hear it."

"That's not going to stop bad things from happening, Honey."

"I know."

We chew in silence, Mom regarding me with sympathy.

"So, is Dad out of town again?"

She nods. "So, who's the guy in question?"

"Mom!"

She grins sheepishly.

"You're as bad as Marcie. Marcie just thinks the guy she likes might like me, but he doesn't like either of us because he only met us today."

It's probably not normal to feel more comfortable opening up to your mother than your friend, but that's the case when it comes to talking with Mom versus Marcie. I guess it's the caring that I sense from Mom. By the time we're eating dessert, I've already told her about the mystifying way I recognized the boy in the wheelchair.

She does not treat it as strange. "Maybe you were born from the same star," she suggests.

"What?"

"Well, I think all of us, at some point, get that feeling of instant connection with someone. There has to be a reason for it." She scrapes up her last bit of pie and pulls out her hair clip. "Maybe it's because the stars aren't just masses of light. Maybe souls are born there. And the souls that break off from the same star keep finding themselves, in life, thrown together, drawn to each other. They may be very different personalities—different ages, races, genders. But something inside them is kindred."

I think about my chemistry homework. It's true that there is a certain order to the way molecules in nature are arranged, the way combinations get repeated. Why wouldn't that apply to people as well?

"Could be. But where is that in the Bible now?" I say teasingly.

We look at each other and laugh.

I try not to think anymore about Marcie's conclusions, but I can't help pondering her words later as I lie in bed replaying the hallway scene over and over again in my mind. It really must have been more than just my

imagination, since even Marcie noticed something strange about it. But of course, being
Marcie, she attributed it to the subject that
takes up ninety-nine percent of her brain cells:
romance.

"Well, she can have him herself," I say to
the darkness. "I couldn't care less."

And then I drift off to sleep, thinking
about his eyes and the way they looked at me.

The dream I slip into is like the day it follows: extraordinary. I'm walking in my back-
yard, and at first I think I'm really there, only
sleepwalking. But I neither feel the autumn
leaves beneath my feet nor hear them crunch,
and though I know the night air must be chilly,
I don't feel cold at all. Instead, I'm filled with
a warmth, a lightness that vibrates all through
me like a delightful tickling from the inside.
Tingling. Moving my legs to walk before I tell
them to, lifting my head up before I decide to
look that way . . .

. . . Until, suddenly, I *am* that lightness—
flying up, up past rooftops, past treetops,
skimming the stars—then feeling a thrill as I
watch the ground grow closer and closer
again. But I don't stop when I hit the ground.
I bounce off it as if it were a trampoline and

soar even higher than before. I'm about to bounce again when I start to get scared. And as soon as I start to panic, the vibration inside me—and with it, the flying—stops.

All I want to do now is sink back into the safety of my bed. As I run for the house, I happen to spot an old wooden comb I lost, lying half-toothless and forgotten in a pile of leaves by the drainpipe.

So that's where I dropped that thing, I think to myself, not picking up the comb in my hurry. I don't even stop to wonder how I pass through the front door without turning the knob and opening it first.

But I do stop when I reach my room and glance in my mirror—and instead of seeing the familiar girl with the big brown eyes and long, curly hair, I see no one. No one at all.

I lean up close to the mirror. Still, no face looks back at me. I swing around and stare across the room. There's someone lying there in my bed—someone with long, curly hair, just like mine.

I try to scream, but I have no throat.

7

Remember Me?

When I awake the next morning, my first thoughts are of the dream; my second, of the boy in the wheelchair. I decide to put my usual shyness aside as best I can and talk to him in school if I get the chance.

But I worry that I won't get the chance. I'm not as good as Marcie is at tracking down boys in the halls of Spring Ridge High before the morning bell rings. I certainly don't want any help from her, though—especially after last night's telephone conversation. Following a quick stop at my locker, I head for the site of yesterday's crash, hoping I don't run into Marcie on the way.

Finding him turns out to be easier than I thought. I catch sight of him down the hallway where Marcie had said his locker was. I guess he sees me before I see him because when I spot him he's already looking at me. It makes me shiver inside—feeling him watch me.

He smiles and shoves a book into his locker.

"Hi," I say. Before I decide to say it.

"Hi," he says, and as I walk past, adds in that strangely familiar voice of his, "Hey— you put a pretty big dent in my wheelchair yesterday."

I half-turn, smiling. "Oh, I did, did I? Where?"

He slaps his locker shut and leans over. "There." He points to an invisible dent near the left wheel.

I squint at it, and he laughs.

"Well, that's nothing compared with the dent that thing put in me," I reply.

"Are you serious? I'm sorry."

"No. It's okay."

I continue walking—slowly, so he can keep up with me.

"My name's Tristan, by the way."

I smile. "I'm Hesper."

"That's a pretty name. I had a friend once named Hesper. A really good friend." His voice sounds kind of hopeful; his eyes search my face—almost expectantly. But for what I do not know.

"Oh. Neat." I watch as his face falls. After

an awkward silence, along with a few of the slowest steps I've ever taken, I say, "So how do you like it here so far?"

His face lights up again. "What do you mean by 'here'?" he asks cautiously. His eyes resume their search.

"What do you mean what do I mean?"

"I mean: what do you *mean?*"

I laugh, and he laughs, too, despite his urgency.

"I mean," I say, "how do you like it here at Spring Ridge High?"

"Oh." He looks away, disappointed. "I like it, I guess. It's a lot different from where I come from, though."

"Where do you come from?"

He hesitates, then says, mostly down to the floor: "It's sort of hard to explain. You might say it's really far away, but then again you might say it's not far away at all."

I frown, trying to think of such a place. "And you might say you've completely lost me!"

Immediately, he glances up. His eyes seem to look not *at* me, but *into* me. "I hope not, Hesper," he says so seriously that it scares me.

For a moment I just stare back at him, too

entranced by his eyes to speak. There's something unearthly about them—their color, their light—yet something very familiar, too.

I want to ask: Who are you? How do I know you? Why do you have that voice? But the only question I can muster is, "So how do you like your classes?"

He starts to answer, then right in the middle of talking about his strict history teacher, heaves an abrupt sigh and says, "Hesper, do you remember me at all?"

"What?" I ask, too surprised to say anything else.

Tristan slows his wheelchair to a stop, and I lean against the wall, hugging my books as a stream of students brushes past.

"I've got to know. I can't stand wondering anymore." His eyes look straight into mine, probing. "Do you get a feeling—even a slight feeling—that you've known me somewhere before?"

"Well, um . . . yes, I do," I say, sawing at my French workbook with my fingernail.

His eyes widen. "You do? What do you remember?"

"Nothing," I say. "Just . . . you."

"What about me?"

I shrug nervously. "I don't know. Your voice—it's just like the voice I've always heard."

He leans forward, excited. "So you could really hear me?"

I nod. "So that voice . . . that was really you?"

"Uh-huh." Beaming, he leans back again. "Go on. What else do you remember?"

"Well, your glow—"

"You can see my glow? Right now—you can see it?"

I nod, feeling as if I'm still stuck in last night's dream.

"You always could see my glow better than anyone else." He's more than excited now—smiling up at me as if I'm some long lost sister instead of a total stranger. Considering how unreal the whole thing is, I wouldn't be surprised if he jumped right out of his wheelchair. "I sure have missed you, Hesper. I've missed arguing with you, bounce-flying with you—and I knew you weren't supposed to remember anything at all, but I couldn't help hoping. . . ."

As he speaks I back away, sliding along the wall for support—or maybe just for assur-

ance that I really am standing in the same ordinary halls of the same ordinary school where
the same ordinary things are supposed to happen. "Wait a minute. What are you talking
about? I really *don't* know you. I mean, I feel
like I should, but I don't, sort of like déjà vu.
I've never met you before."

He nods enthusiastically. "I know: not on
this plane you haven't, but—"

"Wait—just stop, okay? Um. . . ." Sawing
frantically at my workbook, I try to avoid his
eyes. "Look, I've never met you before, and
there's no reason why I should know you."

"Hesper, please—don't be afraid," I hear
him say as I look away into the passing crowd.
"Not of *me.*"

The bell rings. "I'm sorry," I say. "I've
gotta go." I glance quickly at him—his face is
pleading now—and manage a weak smile.
"But it was nice meeting you."

As I rush away, the voice follows me—
calling out my name like it always has, only
this time I know it's the voice of a real person.
"Hesper, I can explain! Meet me here tomorrow morning!"

I pass Marcie on my way back to my
locker.

She looks at me like I'm the one disrupting the balance of this completely normal morning of a completely normal day. "Hesper, where are you going? The bell rang, you know."

"I've just had the craziest conversation of my life, and I'm going home."

"What?"

"I'll call you later, okay? I've got to get out of here before one of the hall monitors catches me."

"Well, okay. Bye." She speaks reluctantly, like she's afraid to leave me alone.

I shove my books into my bag and sneak out the door downstairs by the gym. As I run down the street, I tell myself that everything will return to normal once I reach the safety of home. Mom will be at work, I'll have the whole house to myself, I'll relax and calm down, and nothing out of place will happen. Ever again.

Soon I see the comforting sight of my own driveway. But instead of heading straight for the front door, I find myself circling the house, slowing to a walk after I reach the backyard. Birds hop and fly out of my path. Squirrels scamper about in graceful jerks, dancing their stilted ballet. Leaves crunch and the wind whips, crisp and gentle, at my hair, blowing a few tendrils in my face. I smile, take in a deep breath of delicious autumn air. Everything is as it should be again.

I start walking back to the house, but catching sight of the drainpipe, jump as if I've come face-to-face with a snake.

For there, lying exactly as it was in my dream, is the wooden comb I lost.

8

A Place to Talk

I take the comb to school with me the next day. It's a dumb thing to do, I know. I don't intend to use it, even though I did wash it. So why do I risk missing the bus, rush back inside, and inspire one of Mom's "don't run through the house with your shoes on" lectures just to stuff an old, half-toothless comb into my purse? I don't know. Maybe I just need some tangible proof that my dream really was real. Maybe I'm afraid if I leave that proof lying on my dresser I'll come home to find it isn't there anymore.

I decide to avoid Tristan—to go nowhere near him and ignore him if he comes anywhere near me. But somehow I find this impossible to do once I reach school and see him sitting, wheelchair against the wall, at the very spot where I left him yesterday. He looks so out of place and so alone, watching students zip by with the envy of someone who isn't

allowed to join in their game. I tell myself that
he's crazy, that everything he said was crazy,
that I'm pretty crazy myself for recognizing
someone I've never even seen before.

But something inside me says: No.

Something inside urges me on. Something
guides me up to him even as my common
sense protests.

When Tristan sees me, he smiles, relieved.
"You came."

"No," I say weakly. "Something . . .
brought me."

He shakes his head. *"You* brought you."

Our eyes lock for a moment too long and I
look away, embarrassed. I glance down at my
watch and notice we have about fifteen minutes before the first period bell rings. "Okay,"
I say. "I'm ready to hear what you have to say,
but could you try not to make it too far out this
time?"

He frowns. "Hmm. That might be kind of
hard to do."

I sigh. "Well, could you at least explain
without going on about some past that never
even happened?"

"Okay, I'll try," he agrees, a little deflated.
"But we should talk someplace private. Some-

place outside."

"Outside? Well, there's the courtyard. It's not all that private, but. . . ." Immediately, I regret my suggestion. The courtyard isn't exactly my favorite place to hang out. I've always thought of it as someplace off-limits to students who don't dress like their favorite rock stars, smoke cigarettes for breakfast, or do drugs for lunch.

"Okay. Let's try it," Tristan says.

Reluctantly, I open the door for him and follow him outside into the courtyard, feeling self-conscious for looking so normal. Shaved heads, spiked heads, wild-haired heads all turn our way. I stay close to Tristan—so close that I almost run into him when a boy in a stained shirt jumps in his path and shouts, "Hey, go back where you came from!"

Startled, Tristan rolls himself backwards a little, and I step to his side to avoid the wheels. "Excuse me—do you own the courtyard?" Tristan challenges, glancing from the stained shirt up to the towering boy who wears it.

The boy shakes his head in disgust, then laughs. But his bloodshot eyes do not laugh. "I'm not talking about the courtyard. You don't even get it, do you?"

"Get what?"

The boy stops laughing and leans closer. His eyes are wild and wary—the kind that stare out from shadows in dark forests. "I see what you are. You don't belong here."

Tristan leans forward in his chair. "You're out of your mind."

The boy glances at me. Too late, I try to relax the tension in my face.

"Who's your skinny bird friend?" he jeers.

"Someone *far* above your scorn." Tristan's stare is just as intense as the boy's, but so probing that it makes me wonder if Tristan is peering right inside him. Based on how combative Tristan looks, I half expect him to run over the guy's toes with his wheels.

Then something surprising happens. The boy backs off, and the look I see in his eyes as he does—hatred and fear combined—jolts me with the strongest déjà vu yet. I get a flash of a half-man beast backing off and looking at Tristan in just the same way. It feels like a real memory, though I can't place it. And I still don't understand how or why, but as I follow Tristan back to the door, I sense that I've gotten the explanation I needed, without any logic or persuasion. For I recognize Tristan now as my protector.

I'm glad when we reach the safety of the hallway again. "I wonder what that guy was on," I say.

Tristan shrugs. "Spring Ridge High welcoming committee, I guess."

I smile. "Hope he won't follow us or anything."

"Hesper," he says, his face serious, "there are different ways of sensing things beyond the physical reality. The glow you see because your eyes are sensitive, he sees because his are drugged. There are right ways, wrong ways of tapping into the beyond."

I don't say anything. I mean, I really don't know what to say to that.

We roam the halls a little more before deciding to head for the deserted field across the street. Why I feel safe leaving school grounds with this guy I've practically just met, I don't let myself question anymore. I'm no longer afraid of Tristan, even though he *is* different. Even though he *does* start rolling himself into the street without looking first—and merely watches as the wheels of an oncoming car go skidding to an abrupt halt.

"Hey, watch out!" I yell over the honking.

"We sort of . . . don't have cars where I come from," he explains.

"Where do you come from then—another planet?" I ask.

He looks at me like he wants to say something but doesn't know how to, and the longing in his face awakens a tenderness in me that I'm not quite used to feeling for the other boys at school.

I pick nervously at my French workbook as I cross the street beside him.

"I've never done this before," I say, casting a worried glance at the staid building behind us. "Well, I've skipped class before, but never to put myself on display right across the street from the school. I hope no one sees us."

Luckily, there are a few trees and bushes lining the road. One tree's leaves have all turned yellow, and a blanket of fallen leaves encircles its trunk like a golden shadow. I choose a spot behind the bushes, where I can admire the tree and stay hidden, and take a seat on the hard, cool ground. The weather is just the way I like it: cold enough to chase the bugs away, but not too cold to chase me away.

"Don't worry; they won't see us," he says. Then under his breath: "At least not for long,

I hope."

"What do you mean?"

"You'll see."

I gaze up at him suspiciously, and Tristan smiles. There's a mischief in that smile that makes everything about him seem even more familiar than before. And Marcie's right, too: he is cute. Only it isn't necessarily his features that strike me as attractive. It's the way his glow lights them up from behind, like a bright pebbled path lending color and ripple to the ordinary water passing over it.

I smile back. "So where *are* you from?"

9

A Friend's Sacrifice

"I'm from another plane," Tristan says.

"An airplane? What do you mean?"

"No, I'm talking about a plane as in another dimension of existence. A different place at the same place." He pauses, searching my face for some reaction—and probably seeing the same puzzled look my algebra teacher sees after assigning problems that aren't answered in the back of the book. "I know that doesn't make any sense, but you said you used to hear my voice. I was talking to you from another plane. The same plane you came from."

I get a chill that I can't quite blame on the cool ground. It's an odd sensation, a strong discord between thoughts and feelings.

"Hesper, I don't mean to scare you." Tristan rushes his words, his face mirroring the fear he surely sees in mine. "Please—just hear me out. Trust me. I know you can't remember, and I know why."

"Why then?"

"Because you were Sent here by your kind, and those they Send lose their memory of that plane. They Sent you about a year ago."

"What? That's impossible. I've lived here sixteen years, not one. I remember it."

"You think you remember it, but those are false memories."

I straighten up, defensive. "That makes no sense."

Tristan keeps explaining like a patient teacher who finds nothing strange about it at all. "Being Sent causes a temporary tear in the plane you enter. But it's like cutting through water: life on the plane adjusts all around the tear, erasing it. Life—your consciousness and everyone else's—flows on with as little disruption as possible. Part of that adjustment means you and some others get false memories."

This doesn't satisfy me, but I move on. "So why was I Sent?"

"To help the human plane because it's troubled."

"Ha! You don't need to tell me it's troubled. The nightly news is like a real-life horror movie. I'd love to help, but how can I? I'm just a teenage girl. They should have Sent some old guy with lots of money."

He smiles sadly. "Living here has made you cynical." He's leaning forward in his wheelchair, watching me. Again I get the distinct feeling he's looking *into* rather than *at* me with those unearthly eyes of his. And for a moment I find myself wishing Marcie were right about him liking me.

I try not to abandon logic altogether. "Okay, assuming what you're saying is true— which I'm not assuming—why didn't you forget that plane when they Sent you here?"

"They didn't Send me. I rode the interplane here myself."

"The interplane?"

He sighs and rubs his forehead. "I wish you remembered!" His frustration touches me; it's definitely genuine. "The interplane connects the planes. It's not a physical place like the planes. It's in the spirit realm."

"So how did you get here without forgetting?"

Tristan grows solemn. "Well, the night before they Sent you, we watched them Send someone else. So I sort of learned from that. But then. . . ." He looks down at his legs. "Hesper, I wanted so badly to find you. You were my best friend, and it was all my fault that they Sent you. I didn't care what it took."

"What do you mean? What did it take?"

A pensive expression crosses his face. "You can't ride the interplane without sacrificing part of yourself. But it doesn't have to be your memory you sacrifice." He lightly touches his knees. "I found out something the Alulas don't know. If you're willing to sacrifice any part of your body, you can ride the interplane and keep your memory intact."

I glance at his knees and look back up, horrified. "You gave up your legs?"

He shrugs. "It was worth it . . . to find you."

I stare at him, amazed. Amazed at him for doing what he did, amazed at myself for actually wanting to believe he did it for me. "It wasn't a hang gliding accident? It was the interplane?"

"Hesper, so much has happened since you've been gone," he says with increasing intensity. "There's so much I have to tell you. I can't explain why—at least, not yet—but I need your help. Please, Hess . . . come back with me!"

His words hit me in an urgent flurry: exciting, alarming. "What?" My heart pounds as I slide away.

"The plane you came from is in trouble, and it's because of this plane," he says, pointing to the ground. "Don't you want to help?"

"Of course, but I—I can't even help people *here*, let alone on another plane!" I exclaim, upset at both my helplessness and my own fear of trying. "I don't have any power to help anyone." Shaking, I gather my books, swing my purse over my shoulder, and get to my feet. "I'm already missing first period, and I can't skip two days in a row. I have a test today, too—sixth period history."

"I know you have a life here now, a family. I'm not asking you to leave for good. But Hesper, at the time they Sent you, you were like *my* only family."

I look into his pleading eyes and marvel at the way they affect me. At the way they draw me in with their light, sending my stomach fluttering like a moth entranced.

I force my gaze elsewhere. "I'm sorry, but I can't just take off to some other plane." I shrug apologetically and start for the road, but stop as soon as I hear Tristan speak again.

"You haven't changed a bit, have you, Hesper? Always wanting to do the practical thing—the safe thing; never wanting to do anything daring. Come on, Hesper! Aren't you at least a little curious?"

I sigh and turn around. "What do you want me to do—go with you and forget everything I know here?"

"No, not at all. If you sacrifice your body when you go there, you'll remember everything you forgot. Then, when you ride the interplane back here, sacrifice your memory. The damage to your body will be undone, and you'll be just as you are now, remembering this plane and not the other. You'll have some false memories of the time you were gone, though."

I frown. I can almost feel my brain starting to hurt by now. "But I don't even have any proof of that plane!"

"Look at me: I'm proof," he says. "Anyway, can't you have faith?"

I stand in silent indecision, my mind and my feelings still out of sync.

"Okay, look," he says, "on the other plane

I gave you a comb. I made it out of wood. Did you keep it?"

Catching my breath, I sift through the junk in my purse for the half-toothless wooden comb.

When I hold the comb up, Tristan smiles broadly and says, "Too bad you didn't take better care of it. I can see your hair still needs help."

I don't react to his teasing because I'm too overwhelmed with relief, my mind finally satisfied, my feelings proven true. "I've had this thing for a while. I don't remember how I got it."

"Do you want to remember?"

Nervously, I run my fingers along the comb's scant teeth. "Yes."

"All right!" Tristan says. "Now *that's* the Hesper I know."

10

Riding the Interplane

"So, where do we ride this interplane anyway?" I ask.

"This is fine. Just so it's someplace open and outside."

I step a few paces closer. "Why? I'd rather we go inside my house where no one can see."

"Well, riding it inside a room is dangerous because of the interplanar drift factor. While you ride the interplane, your body is in a vulnerable state. It's not fully on this plane anymore, but it's not quite on the other yet either. And it doesn't stay still: it drifts around—half here, half not here. But it's still enough here that if it drifts inside a wall, it might actually get stuck there."

I wince at the thought of this, even though it sounds far-fetched. *Really* far-fetched. Far down the road, past the state line, past the U.S. border, past the Atlantic Ocean-fetched. Feeling a need to stall for time, I carefully set my books, purse, and comb down on the ground in front of me. "When you go back—and sacrifice your body again—are you going to lose something else? An arm or something?"

He laughs. "Oh, no. I won't lose anything else. My legs will just stay this way. But I could have them return to normal if I rode the interplane and let myself forget."

"Only you don't want to."

"No. Not ever," he says, becoming serious again. "Now close your eyes and try to empty your mind of all thoughts, all worries. Put your trust in . . . what do you call the Great Alula on this plane? I forget."

I open my eyes and notice his are closed. "The who?"

Opening his eyes: "The One you worship. The One you return to when you die."

"You mean God?"

"That's right: God. You still believe in Her, right?"

"Him," I correct.

"Her, Him, whatever. If you want to get technical about it," he says, "I don't think God is a Her *or* a Him, but do you believe in God?"

"Yes. But why does that matter?"

"Well, like I said, the interplane is in the

spirit realm. So to get there you need to trust in what you call God. Think of the way a stream flows—how it rushes down its path without even trying. Now think of that path as God. If you let go and put your trust in the path, there's something in you that flows, like the stream, wherever the path guides it."

His explanation has the same effect on me as his glow. Like magic, it doesn't quite make sense. But it fills me with wonder. It sends a shiver through me. And it doesn't earn my belief; it somehow demands it.

I nod. "Okay. Let's go."

He closes his eyes again. "Now just relax. Trust."

I try to do as he says, but as soon as I do, I feel inside me that same vibration—that same incredible lightness—I felt in my dream. It startles me, so I stop.

"Hesper, it doesn't work if you're afraid. You don't want to end up on the wrong plane. Just let go."

I take a deep breath. Tristan starts talking again, only this time not to me. "Great Alula," he says, "God, Eternal One of many names, please take us safely to the plane of our choosing: the Alula plane."

I take another deep breath. Hesitate. Then slowly, I let go. The vibration comes again, stronger this time: moving my arms to reach out before I tell them to. Lifting my head up before I decide to look that way. Making my heart laugh without any reason for joy. . . .

Tristan is still talking, now about our willingness to sacrifice any part of our bodies, instead of our memories, for the sake of riding the interplane. His voice grows fainter and fainter as inside I grow lighter and lighter—so light, so tingly, I think I could fly if it weren't for my body holding me back. For something is pulling at me—not the physical outer me, but the vibrating inner me. I'm drawn up and forward with such force that I slam down my foot for grounding and hear a crunch as I step on something hard and brittle. My comb! I start to look down for it, then realize I'm no longer standing on it. No longer standing on . . . anything. Just bobbing up and down in a soothing, whirring darkness—partly lifted up by the pull, partly weighed down by my body dragging somewhere beneath me—until all of a sudden, I hit it: the source of the pull. The interplane. And in an instant, I'm freed of the weight and floating.

11

The Problem of Bounce-Flying

I am a lightness,
An emptiness that is full,
A nothing that is everything,
A vibration that is life and joy and flight.
I am the beat without the heart,
The thought without the mind,
The song without the voice,
And amidst forgetfulness, I am that which
never forgets. . . .

"Hess?"

I open my eyes with a start. My arms feel sore, and my whole body suddenly seems as restrictive as a tight shoe. My first thoughts are, *I've stepped on my comb; I've smashed it.* But then it all comes back to me—what I heard in the silence . . . saw in the darkness . . . felt with no senses. And I look around me in awe.

I find myself standing exactly like I was, only no longer *where* I was. The ground beneath my feet is soft and spongy—perfect for bounce-flying. The air is not cold but cool; the sky, not so much white with clouds as spotted brown with skymounts. And the person so anxiously observing me is not a boy in a wheelchair, but a boy with a horse's body from the waist down—and four of the scrawniest hoofed legs I've ever seen.

A shimmer of happiness shoots up through me, catching somewhere between my throat and my heart.

"Tris!" I cry. "I remember!"

His face breaks into a smile. "I knew it! I knew it would work!"

"I remember! I remember!" Laughing, I jump up and down, delighting in the familiar spring of the soil, dancing around in dizzy circles while the sound of Tristan's laughter fills my ears.

Tristan's laughter. Tristan.

I stop and look at him in silent amazement.

"You . . . came for me," I breathe, admiring how much taller and stronger he looks now than he did the day of our parting, in spite of his thin legs. "And you didn't give up—

even when I treated you like you were a stranger."

He gazes at me intently. "I told you we'd see each other again. Remember?"

I sigh in feigned annoyance. "Of course I remember! I remember it all!" I lift up my wings and twirl around, giddy with renewed excitement. It isn't until I fall back on the springy ground and wait for the world to stop its spinning that I notice the peculiar look on Tristan's face.

I sit up, leaning back on my wings. "What is it?"

Tristan's voice is unusually weak. "Your arms. . . ."

The bottoms of my feet prickle. Somehow, even before I look for my arms, I know they're not there. It's the strangest sensation. Up until now, I've felt arms where arms would be, but as soon as I stop and think about it, I realize I'm only feeling what *should* be, not what really *is*.

"The interplane sped up your arms' growth into your wings," Tristan says as I practically jump to my feet, looking from the underside of one wing to the other, still not quite able to register it. My arms are completely gone, the bones fused with those of my wings. There's nothing left but a bit of pink skin showing here and there through the pale brown feathers.

"But look!" The stomp of Tristan's hoof draws my eyes back to him. "My legs . . . I can feel them. They look terrible, but they're not nearly as bad anymore!" He shakes his legs around, smiling yet confused. "I thought I'd never be able to feel them again unless I let myself forget." He glances down at his legs, then up at where my arms should be.

I wrap my wings around me self-consciously.

"Hey, don't. You look beautiful." His compliment is not something I have time to savor, for he quickly adds, "Besides, with all that hair, who would know you don't have arms?"

My wings fly out indignantly. But there are no hands to put on my hips.

He smiles. "That's better." He says it in his same old teasing way, but there's a soft look in his eyes that sends a thrill warming through me.

"Really!" I say with a playful smile. "You know, it's a good thing I didn't lose my wings.

Then we couldn't go bounce—" All at once, it hits me. I gasp. "Oh, no! We still can't go bounce-flying!"

Tristan echoes my gasp. "You're right! You need arms to hold onto me, and"—he lifts one of his scrawny legs—"I need strong legs to bounce on."

The truth of his words makes my stomach lurch like a broken wing. "Oh, no! I want to bounce-fly so badly."

"I know—me, too."

"It's not fair!" I exclaim. "Why do we have to lose the parts we need most?"

Tristan shakes his head in frustration. "I don't know, Hess." He looks down and paws at the ground with a frail front hoof. "I wish we could pick the part we want to give up, but it doesn't work that way. I guess remembering is more costly than I thought."

"What's the good of remembering bounce-flying if we can't even do it?" I grumble. "It's torture."

Tristan's head jerks up. "Well, at least *you* can still fly. You've still got your wings, you know. I've been looking forward to bounce-flying again for a long time."

Listening to him, an image comes to my

mind—an image of Tristan sitting all alone in his cave: shunned by the Mantaurs because of his glow, left with nobody to bounce-fly with, nobody to talk to except someone on another plane who might not even hear him. The image is quite sobering. I was the one Sent, but it was Tristan who was truly isolated. I was re-united—albeit unknowingly—on the human plane with my real mom, for with my memo-ries restored, I know that my caring human mom and the Alula mom who was Sent from me are one and the same. Tristan, on the other hand, was deprived of the only companion he had.

"Oh, Tris. . . ."

"I thought there might be other things you'd be glad to remember." He looks back down. Quietly: "Other things besides bounce-flying."

"There are. You know there are."

He continues pawing silently at the mossy ground. I want to tell him I care much more about him than bounce-flying, but I find the words too hard to say. I want to pat him on the shoulder, but I feel helpless to do it without a hand. I want to give him a hug, but somehow, I'm afraid of how good it would feel—to have his arms around me.

With a resolute kick of his hoof, Tristan looks up. The expression on his face is all too familiar: it's the same one I always used to see right before he got me to do something I didn't really want to do. "Hey!" he says. "Let's try it anyway!"

"What?"

"We can't be sure we can't bounce-fly unless we try it. So, let's try it! We could use the vines in my cave to tie you to my back, and then it's just a matter of my legs."

I roll my eyes. "Are you kidding?"

"Aw, come on, Hess. Maybe we could do it!"

"Yeah—and maybe we could drop on our heads."

Even though I know I'm right, there's no time to argue my point. By the time I say "heads," Tristan is already galloping as fast as his skinny legs can carry him in the direction of his cave. I run after him, yelling for him to wait. Of course, he doesn't. He just glances over his shoulder and grins.

I swear, sometimes Tristan can be so exasperating.

12

The Sun is the Same

The sight of Tristan's cave makes me forget, for a moment, all about bounce-flying. And all about the danger in visiting the forbidden ground in broad daylight, for any Alula or Mantaur to see.

Like everything else, the cave is exactly as I remember it, yet at the same time just as new and marvelous as a familiar stone discovered to be a jewel. With its rounded, moss-coated roof, it looks less like the caves I've learned about in school and more like a hill with a hole in the side of it. Never before have I thought anything of this. Or of the surrounding landscape's many hills and few trees. Or of the skymounts' likeness to giant clumps of earth frozen in mid-fall. But I notice it all now and miss it all, too, though the time for missing has passed—and I have missed it.

When I reach the cave, I know it by smell alone: that mossy, moist smell that, on the human plane, might be the scent of my own backyard, fresh with the aftertaste of rain. Flashing an eager smile, Tristan pulls up one of the vines growing along the back wall. "Come on! Let's do some flying."

"Tris, you're crazy!"

"We'll see. Climb onto my back."

As Tristan loops the vine around us, I let my eyes wander over my favorite old place to sneak away to. The inside of the cave is just as soft and smooth as I remember it. There are no stalactites, no stalagmites—like the ones I've seen in science books—shooting out from the ceiling and floor. Only branches draped with clothes jutting out from one side of the cave. I smile. I remember bringing those branches down from the skymounts. And those Holy Tablets, too. The ones I'd thought he should have, since the Mantaurs don't have any of their own, the beasts, and wouldn't give him one even if they did.

But despite these familiar objects, there's still something very different about the cave. Tristan's clothes are hung more neatly than usual. His wooden carvings are arranged too carefully at the table where he created them. The sleeping cloak is not carelessly thrown

back but folded over with care, as smooth as
the carpet nailed to my bedroom floor on the
human plane. Even the way the moss grows,
undisturbed, along a ground once marred by
prints and circle patterns of restless hooves,
tells me Tristan has not lived here in quite
some time.

How long has he been gone looking for
me, I wonder?

"Okay, now tell me if this is too tight,"
says Tristan. Then he pulls the vine so tight I
can hardly breathe.

"Too tight!"

"Hess, it has to be tight or it won't work."

"Well, why did you ask me then?"

"Oh, okay," he says, loosening it.

I look over his shoulder as he ties the knot.
"It feels incredible—riding the interplane.
Like being gradually pulled out of your body
and then thrown back into it again."

"Well, that's pretty much what happens.
You're drawn in by the interplane's pull, but
until you reach it, you still have a strong connection to your body. So your body drags
along, and that's what causes the interplanar
drift factor. Then when you hit the interplane,
it separates you from your body until you

reach the next plane."

I think about how it felt to rise up as a lightness, and my insides tingle at the memory. "It's almost like flying, only without the wings."

"Hey, that's a good way of putting it."

He turns to smile at me, and I realize how close our faces are. I can tell he realizes it, too, because he stops smiling and grows thoughtful, studying me fondly. When his eyes stray down to my lips and he leans in closer, my stomach starts bounce-flying on its own. I feel sure he's about to kiss me, and I want him to, but he stops short, his affectionate look replaced by anxiety, as if he's caught himself doing something wrong. He turns around hastily.

His behavior leaves me flustered but too embarrassed to question it. "Well, come on," I say. "Let's get this over with."

To gather enough momentum, we gallop a long distance before taking off, but I can still tell right away it isn't going to work. Tristan's transformed legs feel much less sturdy beneath me, and it's a lot more awkward flapping my wings with only a vine and my out-of-shape leg muscles to keep me balanced on my jostling seat. When Tristan leaps into the air and we head up, it feels nothing like our usual jump-soaring. It's more like an upward tripping, a desperate lunging. The stress of it breaks the vine with a stinging snap and sends Tristan toppling to the ground. As he rises to his feet, dazed but determined, I alight beside him, not knowing whether to check for injuries or laugh.

"Are you okay, Tris?"

"Yeah. Let's try it again."

I stare. "What!"

"Come on. All we have to do is get a thicker vine."

The next vine we use is thicker, but that doesn't stop it from coming loose just as we brace for our first bounce. Luckily for Tristan, we aren't too high off the ground when the rough pressure around my waist gives out and he falls to the ground again with a thump.

Tristan finally solves the vine problem by using several of them, wrapping them tighter, and tying them with multiple knots. But that doesn't do anything to solve the problem of Tristan's legs. When at last we make it to our first bounce without falling, his two front legs buckle under him the moment we hit the ground, sending us literally falling on our faces.

"Ow!" I yell. "Untie the vines! I can't move."

"Get your hair out of the way. I can't see."

"Untie the vines first," I insist.

"How can I if I can't see?"

We break down laughing. "My hair is stuck," I say. "Lift your head."

We're lying on our side, Tristan's weight pressing on my leg. I move my hair away, and he struggles to untie the knots, tickling me on purpose in the process so I laugh even harder. With my free foot, I get him back under his forelegs where I know he's most ticklish. Writhing, he reaches behind and wraps his arms around me, sending my insides bouncing and soaring again as he lifts up on his legs and rolls me gently to his other side so I'm facing him. Our laughter lingers.

"Well, that was almost as fun as the real thing," I declare, lying back on the soft ground and smiling up at the sky.

"Hey, maybe if we tried to—"

I silence him with a you've-got-to-be-kidding-me look, then gaze back up at the sky. For minutes we're both quiet, except for our breathing. I study the skymounts, feeling as small as a fish looking up at lily pads from the bottom of a pond. I search for flits of Alulas and frown, wondering why I don't see any. And then—all of a sudden—the flash of something silvery white catches my eye. It appears and disappears in an instant, winking in and out of existence as fast as the sad cry of a voice from nowhere. And before I can sit up or even gasp, I'm left blinking up at the empty blue patch in the sky, wondering:

Did I just see an *airplane* there?

No, of course not. It couldn't have been. I shake my head and smile to myself. Some sort of post-interplanar travel hallucination, I suppose. Or maybe just the sun playing tricks on me.

Still a little shaken, I give the sun a quick skim—and for the first time, realize it doesn't look any different on this plane than it does on the other.

I turn to Tristan, only to see him already watching me. I feel a warmth suffuse my cheeks and hope it isn't flushing them too pink.

"Tris, it's funny how the sun looks the same. Do you think it only has one plane?"

"No. The sun has a different form on each of the different planes, just like our planet. It only looks the same because it gives off heat on both this plane and the human one." He gazes at the sky, squints. "Actually, the sun gives off some type of heat on all the planes—except the barren one."

"So that's why nothing grows on the barren plane."

"Yeah. Because on the plane where our planet is barren, the sun is cold."

I frown. "Hmmm."

"It's the same way with the moon, you know. And the planets. They all take different forms on different planes. And they all have different beings on different planes, too. Only their planes with life don't always correspond to our planes with life. So when we look at a planet, what we see is its barren plane. And when the beings on that planet look at us, what they see is our barren plane."

"Oh, I get it. You mean that from the outside looking on, our planet *appears* as deserted to other planets as other planets *appear* to us." I think about the astronauts and how much they risk just to visit the moon's barren plane, just to take pictures of Mars's barren plane. If only they knew about the interplane.

I sit up with a start. "Hey! Where did you hear about all this, anyway?"

But Tristan does not answer. He's too busy now looking up at the sky—or rather, at something *in* the sky. Remembering my "airplane," I quickly follow his gaze.

"Tris, what is it?"

At first I think the small dot coming from the skymount above us is an Alula out for a fly. But then I notice how fast it's flying—not across the sky, but straight down. And as the dot gets closer and closer, bigger and bigger, I start to make out not only the broad wings of an Alula, but with growing disbelief, the four strong legs of a Mantaur.

13

Council of the Alulas

"Like I said, Hess, *a lot* has happened since you've been gone," I hear Tristan say as I stare, incredulous, up at the sky.

"But . . . ?"

"I was about to tell you. I was—really."

Mouth agape, I watch the Alula and the Mantaur as they soar gracefully to the ground, just the way we used to. They bounce-gallop to a landing a mere few paces in front of us, and Tristan and I hasten to our feet. The Alula flips back her straight, black hair and slides off the Mantaur, looking as amazed to see me as I am to see her. I recognize her as the Alula who saw us that night of the Sending—the Alula who told the Council on me. She's staring at me in that same striking way of hers, her brown eyes wide with awe.

The Alula approaches us gingerly, almost as if she's afraid to get too close. The Mantaur follows, his eyes on Tristan and narrowing with such open hatred that I wish poor Tristan didn't have a glow, even though it's so lovely.

The Alula is the first to speak. "You've returned," she says to me. "They said you might, but I never believed them."

"Who?" I ask.

"The Council, of course."

I shudder involuntarily.

"They're waiting for you."

"Waiting for me?" I echo.

She steps closer, looking me over as if I'm a miracle she still can't quite believe. "Has the interplane erased your memory? Have you forgotten your great duty? Do you even know who you are?"

Her eyes rest on my wings, and I wrap them around myself, hoping she hasn't noticed the premature aging of my arms. "I remember everything," I say coldly. *No thanks to you.*

Her mouth drops open. *"Every*thing? But how? The interplane—"

"Just tell her the message," the Mantaur cuts in, scowling for the first time at me instead of Tristan.

She glares at him. "All right." Straightening a little, she resumes her formal tone. "The Council will meet with you. Now."

I step a little closer to Tristan and shake my head. "They're not Sending me again. I'm not going back yet." For once I wish I could be more like Marcie and say exactly what I'm thinking. Then I'd tack on a "you witch" at the end of the sentence.

"Do you have any idea how valuable you are to them? They won't want to Send you back. You're the first Alula ever to return from a Sending. To ride the interplane and remember."

Out of the corner of my eye, I see Tristan inch closer to me. It makes me feel better, knowing he's there.

"The Council is waiting," she says before climbing onto the Mantaur's back. "Follow us."

I turn to Tristan in panic.

"Wait," Tristan says. "Give us a minute." He takes my wing and guides me aside. His voice lowers to a whisper. "Hess, they're going to want to know how you rode the interplane back here. Don't tell them."

"Why not?"

"Remember how I told you I needed your help? This has something to do with it. I'll explain afterward. But whatever you do, *don't* tell about sacrificing our bodies instead of our memories."

"Well, all right," I whisper uncertainly.

"Just let them think you've lost your arms the same way all Alulas do."

I nod, hugging myself with my wings. It's true that in rare cases Alulas puzzle everyone by losing their arms while they're still quite young. I never thought I'd be one of them, though.

"I'll be waiting at my cave," Tristan says. "Be careful, Hess."

"Okay."

I see the concern on his face and wonder how anyone could have cause to hate him. I have no hands for him to hold steady like he used to, but the pressure of his fingers against my wing feels just as warm, just as good.

"I'm ready now," I say to the Alula and Mantaur.

As I fly behind them, I can't look up at our destination; I can only look down at Tristan's upturned face, watching it get smaller and smaller, wishing I didn't have to fly alone. It isn't until I hear the Alula yell, "Hurry up!" that I realize how terribly out of shape I am. Breathing hard, I struggle to close the fast-growing gap between the two bounce-fliers and me. By the time I finally land on the jarring skymount and flip my hair back off my face, I'm panting like I've run the mile in gym class.

The sight of Mantaurs all over the skymount is quite a shock. They seem to have made themselves at home, although they act more subdued than I would expect: most are lying lazily in the fields or tossing rocks at animals; a few are fighting each other for sport. The Alulas have always had nothing to do with the Mantaurs except when they've absolutely had to—about once every year, at the Merging. But here they are now—Mantaurs on a skymount!—looking as incongruous as demons in heaven, lounging around plotting their crimes.

The scowling Mantaur trots off to join the other Mantaurs, and soon dozens of astonished Alulas—some familiar, some not—turn and look my way. More than ever I feel like a girl, not an Alula, lost in a strange world full of beings hostile to me.

"Why is the Council on such a low skymount?" I ask the Alula as she throws back a door to the interior.

"The Council members moved here from the High Skymount after they Sent you. Here, they could keep an eye on the . . . Boytaur."

I don't like the way she says "Boytaur." I don't like it at all.

As I follow her below the surface, I can't help thinking how crude the stairway seems compared with the stairs at school, how much the familiar smell of my old home reminds me of garden soil, part of a more recent home. I can almost feel my missing hands tremble, remembering the last time I walked down one of these dim tunnelways, the last time I met with the Council. Now there's one experience I would not mind forgetting: listening to the Council tell me about the evil aliens, my "great duty," and, worst of all, the emergency Sending planned for me that very night.

All too soon, the Alula stops and knocks at a wide door that opens to a slightly brighter room full of more staring faces. Only this time the faces are older, less surprised to see me. And more full of the cold pride so typical of the Alulas.

"She says she remembers everything," the Alula informs the Council.

"Thank you, Nitza," says the silver-haired

Alula at the far end of the long, ornate table. "You may leave now."

Nitza, as I now know the Alula is called, gives me one last look before leaving me alone with the Council. Her brown eyes shine no longer with awe, but with envy. The silver-haired Alula—the one I remember as the Council Wing—invites me to take the seat at the end opposite her. I sink into the seat, thinking how much I would love to switch places with Nitza and be the one heading down the tunnelway instead of staying.

The Council Wing brushes back a long strand of her hair and smiles at me. I smile back, warily. "Hesper, my child," she says, "we are very grateful for your return." Rows of gray- and white-haired heads nod their agreement. "We have many questions to ask you, but I think it only fair that we first answer your questions. No doubt you were taken aback by the sight of Mantaurs on the sky-mount. Let me explain why you saw this.

"As you know, the balance of the planes is as delicate as the waters of the creek. You cannot poison the single-celled creatures without poisoning the creatures on the next level who depend on them and, in turn, those on the

next level who depend on them. These aliens
with their presence on our planet are having
the same chain effect on the planes. They
came first to the human plane and disrupted it.
Then they spread to the barren plane. But they
do not even need to go to the other planes to
harm them as well. For remember the Poem of
the Planes: 'Should one plane slip, then each
shall fall.'

"Their presence is disrupting our plane—
through no fault of our own, but because what
is wrong taints what is right. The aliens have
made the awareness on the human plane too
much like the awareness on our plane. And
now what we dreaded most is coming to pass:
our plane and the human plane are blending
into one.

"Already we are feeling the beginnings of
this blending. Interplanar leaks have formed,
and through these leaks drift deadly beings
from the human plane. Six flits of Alulas have
been struck by huge, shiny beings with wings
that fly without flapping. They soar out from
nowhere, then vanish."

I feel my muscles tighten, remembering
the airplane I saw—for indeed it must have
been an airplane after all.

"Even more Mantaurs have been hit by monsters of the ground: roaring, fuming beings with round legs that run so fast they roll. They, too, come without warning, then vanish."

I think of that car accident Marcie told me about over the phone—the one where the lady swore she'd hit a "man on a horse." And it all makes sense to me now.

"Those aren't beings," I break in. "The ones in the sky are called airplanes, and the ones on the ground are called cars. The people there sit inside them, and the airplanes and cars take the people where they want to go. You see, humans don't have wings like we do, and they can't run fast like the Mantaurs."

The Alulas listen intently, the fascination clear on their faces "My child," the Council Wing says, nodding her approval, "the danger of these aliens is so great it has driven us to do something we never thought possible: unite with the Mantaurs. The large numbers of these cars, as you call them, make them a bigger threat to the ground than the . . ."

"Airplanes," I fill in.

". . . are to the skies. So we have made an agreement with the Mantaurs. We let them

stay on the surfaces of our skymounts in exchange for their help in fighting the aliens and
their promise not to attack us or the animals of
our skies. We know they do not intend to keep
their promise, so for our safety we must spray
them each night with the Merging herb. We
cannot keep them drowsy forever, but what
else can we do? We *must* have their help. For
only with their help—and yours—can we rid
our planet of the aliens."

"But what can *I* do?"

She smiles. "First, answer all of our questions. You can do that, can you not?"

I fix my gaze down on the table. "Well,
umm . . . I'll try."

Her voice sounds much colder without the
smiling face to go with it. "For your sake and
the sake of your two planes, I hope you will
try very hard. Moira?"

A new voice draws my eyes to an Alula
resembling a much older Nitza. "Hesper, the
Mantaurs tell us the Boytaur has a greenish
glow about him. Can you see this glow?"

"Yes. Can't you?"

"No. You seem to be the only Alula who
can."

The Alula beside her speaks next. "The

Boytaur brought you back, did he not?"

It's more of a statement than a question, but I find myself nodding anyway.

"And he is able to ride the interplane without forgetting."

This time it's entirely a statement. I let my silence be my affirmation.

All around me, Alulas exchange knowing glances. "Are you aware that no other Mantaurs are capable of riding the interplane at all?" Moira asks.

I give her a nervous shrug. "He did watch that Sending with me."

"My child," cuts in the Council Wing, "any other Mantaur would still not be able to ride the interplane."

I look back down at the table. "Oh."

"So, since the Boytaur brought you back," says Moira, "he must have told you how he learned to ride the interplane—and to ride it without forgetting."

"Well. . . ." I look up to see two rows of wrinkled faces leaning forward in eager anticipation. "He said he figured it out, that's all."

"But he must have taught you how to do it."

I hesitate. I can see there's no use lying: they know very well he must have taught me or else I wouldn't even be here, wouldn't even remember them. But it is with reluctance that I manage a "Yes."

"Good!" says the Council Wing. "And now you will teach us."

They all smile at each other, and some flutter their wings in excitement. Then they turn back to me expectantly.

In a small voice I say, "I'm sorry. I can't do that."

Their smiles fade as fast as memories erased by the interplane. The Council Wing leans forward with controlled calm, but her wings fly out stiffly behind her. *"What?"*

"I'm sorry. I—I just can't," is my timid reply.

And above all the gasps, all the whispers, all the cries of surprise, I hear the Council Wing say, slowly and deliberately: "Oh, yes, my child. I think you can."

14

Tristan's Secret

The Alulas fall silent as their leader continues. "This knowledge," she says, "could be the key to saving two whole planes from a blending that would destroy them both—and all the planes, eventually. Do you understand that, my child? This knowledge could save everyone—including yourself! What possible reason can you have for keeping it from us?"

"I don't understand why it's so important to remember," I say. "I thought you wanted Alulas to forget and spend their lives on the human plane."

"Tell us how to ride the interplane without forgetting," says the Council Wing, "and we will tell you why it is so important."

"I'm sorry. I—I just can't. Not until I talk to Tristan first."

Again, the Council members exchange knowing glances.

"You would trust that Boytaur before you

would your own kind? You would betray your great duty for him? *Why?"* the Council Wing demands.

Her eyes, like two blinding headlights, compel me to look away. "He . . . found me," I explain down to the table. "You Sent me against my will. And now I've returned, and you say you're grateful. But it was Tristan who went searching for me." I force myself to look up at her. At all of them. "Tristan cares about me." I pause, scanning their proud faces —and disliking every one. "You never did."

The Council Wing no longer regards me with anger. Instead, a puzzling mixture of pity and dismay crosses her face. "Oh, my child," she says with a weary sigh, "you have so much to learn." Shaking her head: "So very much to learn."

Her words are too confusing—too frightening—for me to let myself hear them.

Moira speaks next. "Hesper," she says, "we care about you and every other being on every other plane of this planet. That is why we Sent you and why we need your help now."

"Well, if you wanted me to trust you, you shouldn't have Sent me."

The Council Wing says, "We will not Send you again. But we will order you to ride the interplane again." Her words jar me like the slam-hit of a skymount landing after a smooth bounce-flight. She continues, "I told you the aliens have spread to the barren plane. So, to understand why we need the information we ask for, you must visit the barren plane."

I glance around the table in panic as the Council members calmly nod their agreement. "No!" is all I can manage to shout.

The Council Wing says, "If you prefer to share with us your secret to riding the interplane and remembering, we will be happy to go there ourselves."

A rush of heated words runs through my head, but not one syllable reaches my lips. So I just sit there, glaring down at the table top, feeling as helpless as a child ordered to choose between spinach and liver.

"Before we can fight the aliens, we must learn as much as we can about them," I hear Moira explain. "What do they look like? How do they think? How can they be killed? You must find the answers."

The Council Wing adds, "Take the Boytaur with you. Leave as soon as possible, and when you return, report immediately to this Council room."

"Wait!" I say as the Alulas rise to leave. "If these aliens are so evil, how do you know they won't do something horrible to me?"

"They will not," says an Alula, simply. "The Boytaur will be with you."

This answer strikes me as odd, for it's the first time any of the Council members—or anyone on this plane, for that matter—has given Tristan any credit.

"But how do you know I'll even come back?" I persist. "I could just head for the human plane instead."

"And return to what?" asks Moira. "Hesper, we can only guess what a troubled place the human plane must be now. But you know; you have seen it. Can you really go back, knowing you can help, yet doing nothing?"

Her words call up images of the nightly news with its theme of the evil preying on the innocent in an unjust survival of the foulest. I feel my heart constricting. I swallow hard.

"You're right," I say quietly. "I do want to help."

"Good!" the Council Wing cries. "Now

go, and may the Great Alula fan Her wings
above you."

As I fly to the once-forbidden ground—
keeping a close eye out for any drifting airplanes—I try not to focus on the fact that my
wings are so tensed I can hardly flap them,
and concentrate on the fact that I'll be doing
something to help.

But *can* I help, *really?*

Images of the TV news resurface in my
mind: artists' renderings of killers on the
loose, photos of victims smiling from a time
before they were murdered, their bright faces
as eerie as the lights left in the night sky by
stars long gone. The hopelessness of it all
sends a pang through me. I push the images
back down, force myself to stay dry-eyed as I
reach the ground and start for Tristan's cave.
After all, I'm not a little girl anymore, and I
don't want Tristan to see me as a crybaby.
Like my flight, my steps are much more hesi-
tant now that I know about the interplanar
leaks. I can't help wondering how close I am
to the highway by the school. I can't help
wondering if I'm walking right down the middle of it.

Tristan is on the lookout for me outside his

cave. When he sees me, he sighs, relieved. "Are you okay?" His voice is so sympathetic that, against my will, the tears start welling up in my eyes.

I quickly blink them away. "Oh, Tris, I'm in such a big mess."

"Tell me what happened."

He puts his arm around me as we walk inside. It warms me both inwardly and out, and it makes me feel safe, too—like I don't have to worry about being alone. I explain what the Council said about the evil aliens and the blending. Then I point out how curious they were about him and how many questions they asked.

"You didn't tell them how we did it, did you?" he says. "How we sacrificed our bodies instead of our memories?"

"Don't worry, I didn't. But they were definitely mad about that. They need to know how to do it to fight the aliens. Why didn't you want me to tell them?"

With a heavy sigh, Tristan looks down. "I really need to tell you, and I will. But . . . it's hard, Hess. I can't just yet."

I cast him my most annoyed glance. "It seems like nobody can tell anybody anything!

You can't tell me why I couldn't tell them how I rode the interplane back. And because I couldn't tell them, they're forcing me to go to the barren plane. There, they say, I'll find the answers to everything *they* can't tell *me!*" Exhausted and aggravated, I plop down on the soft ground. It bounces me back a little, then gives in under my weight, almost like the cushions of my bed back on the human plane.

Tristan sits down next to me. "Are you serious?" he asks anxiously. "You're really going there—to the plane where nothing grows?"

"Yes, I'm going there," I whisper. "I have to. But you have to go with me."

He nods, enthusiastic. "Sure!"

I look at him in disbelief. "How can you be so eager to go? It's probably awful there!"

Tristan shakes his head. "No, it isn't."

"And the aliens—they're probably hideous-looking—"

Tristan shakes his head. "No, they aren't."

"—and they're so evil! They'll probably do something dreadful to us!"

Tristan shakes his head. "No, they won't."

His confidence is unbelievable: it curdles my fear into fury. "How do you know?" I explode. "You don't know what it's like there!

You think it'll be fun and exciting, right? Just like spying on the Sending! Just like always— adventure now, consequences later. Always, 'Come on, Hess! Let's not think about it first. Let's not worry what'll happen. Let's just go!' " The tears sting like soap burning to be washed out. Against my will, they fall, and I cover my face with my wings.

From inside the dark softness of my feathers, I hear Tristan's voice grow more cautious, more gentle. "Hess? Please. I know what I'm talking about this time." He pauses, takes a deep breath. "All right, I'm going to tell you now. Are you listening?"

I take my wings away from my face and stare, blurry-eyed, down at the sweet-smelling moss.

"What I have to tell you is hard for me to say, and it's going to be hard for you to hear. But you've got to listen to me and try to understand. I do know what it's like there. I know it's not awful. I know they're not hideous-looking. And I know they're not evil."

I lift my head slowly, somehow afraid to meet the bright green eyes that seem more unearthly now than ever before. "But Tris, how do you know?"

He looks at me for a long moment, his face serious. Then he says, "Because I'm one of them."

PART III

The Barren Plane

15

The Presence of Dyaphinees

My first instinct is to laugh and wait for him to tell me he's just kidding. My second instinct is to get up and fly as far away as I possibly can. But I find myself too stunned to do either. Too stunned to do anything but sit and stare at the only friend I ever trusted. The only friend I ever . . . loved.

Tristan, an *alien?* The playful Boytaur I spent my youth bounce-flying with . . . an *alien?* The boy at school I listened to and believed . . . an *alien?* The very thought of it makes me cringe.

"Hess?" Tristan leans closer to me, and I quickly slide away. "Why are you so surprised? You've always seen through my disguise. I've felt it. To you, my skin's as transparent as tissue paper against a sunlit window."

I look into his face. He seems no less kind, no less himself now, but for the first time his bewitching light sends a chill through me. I think of all the times I wondered at that glow, and I shiver, realizing what it is I've been seeing.

"Don't look at me like that!" Tristan says, flinching as if I've struck him.

"Like what?"

"Like. . . ." He rises and turns away. "Like I'm some sort of monster."

"I—I didn't mean to—"

"I know what you're thinking of me," he breaks in, his tail swishing. "I know! But think how it's been for me—knowing what you are. To me you're the alien, you know. Yes: *you,* Hesper. You and every Alula who spies on me, every Mantaur who hates me, every spaced-out human who orders me to leave. Do you think I never felt like shrinking from you just like you shrink from me now?"

The beat of my heart pounds in my head and thunders in my ears. *Knowing what you are,* he had said. *What,* not who. I gulp. I don't know which seems worse to me: the thought of Tristan as an alien or the thought of Tristan thinking of *me* as an alien.

"I'm sorry—I didn't mean that," he says, his anger evaporating into a pained look of regret.

"All this time we've been friends." My voice is as shaken as the rest of me. "Best friends. But you never told me this—even the last time I saw you before my Sending. Remember? I told you what the Council said about the aliens, and you acted like you didn't even know about them."

"I didn't know. Not then."

"What?"

"I didn't know then who I really was," he explains, digging circles in the moss with an agitated right front hoof. "I mean, I knew I didn't fit in, didn't feel comfortable around anyone . . . except you. But it wasn't until after your Sending that I found out why. I spent half a year trying to ride the interplane so I could follow you, but I couldn't do it.

"Then one day an old Mantaur with a limp came to my cave. I'd never seen him before, but he seemed different from the other Mantaurs, and I trusted him right away. Just listening to the sound of his voice, I trusted him. There was a . . . joy in that voice. It made you want to laugh, though there was nothing funny at all." Tristan smiles a little to himself. "He was nice to me. He didn't treat me like a freak the way the other Mantaurs do. And he had a glow even brighter than mine. Bright blue.

"He taught me how to ride the interplane without forgetting. I went to the barren plane with him, and everything came back to me. I remembered my life with the Dyaphinees before they Sent me, as a child." He pauses, looks at me almost apologetically. "I was one of those messengers, Hesper—the ones you said the aliens were Sending. The ones the Alulas said they were trying to stop."

My heart strains under his words, under all the strong and different emotions that they stir inside me.

"The whole revelation was a big shock at first," he continues. "But it didn't take long for me to find out how wonderful it is to live with others who accept you for what you are. I *belonged*. I wasn't an outcast anymore. I could finally live with a group of my own kind." He takes a cautious couple of steps forward, holding me in place with eyes that still send my stomach fluttering. "The only reason I ever left was to find you."

I look down, nervously twisting a strand of curly hair around my finger. "Tristan, do you understand what you and your kind—these

Dyaphinees—are doing to our planet, just by being here?"

"Would you want me to leave?"

I sigh, exasperated. "Of course not, but—"

"I understand what the Alulas told you about us, if that's what you mean. But that isn't the truth." He pauses, studying me. "You believe me, don't you?"

"Oh, Tristan, I don't know anymore! I'm too confused."

"Then I'll prove it to you. Come on," he says and heads out of the cave.

"No, wait." I follow close behind. "I don't want to go there yet. I need to wait a while."

He slows his canter but doesn't stop. "Is that what the Alulas said—to wait a while?" he says over his shoulder.

"No, but—"

"Well, come on, then."

"But—"

He halts and turns around. Too abruptly. Too soon for me to prevent myself from bumping right into him and then immediately jumping back. Instinctively, like a hand retracting before the burn is felt.

I don't see the hurt in his face. It's there, I know, but I don't see it because I don't look at his face.

The quiver in his voice startles me. "Hesper, it's me. Tristan. Your *friend*, remember?"

Silence. Just me and my best friend, the complete stranger, and this silence looming between us.

"Of course I remember," I say down to his hooves. "You know I remember everything."

We continue, Tristan with purpose, myself with reluctance—not just because of our destination, but because of the interplanar leaks that, any moment, could send a car zooming out at us from the human plane. My anxiety over this leaves me, though, when Tristan steers away from several stakes driven crookedly into the ground.

"The Mantaur with the blue glow put those there," he explains, "to mark off the place on the human plane where the road runs by the school."

Tristan lopes along for a greater distance than necessary, perhaps for my sake, perhaps because he isn't as eager to go to the barren plane as he acts. But the Mantaurs' territory, with its dearth of trees and absence of buildings, is ideal for riding the interplane, and wide-open space surrounds us long before

Tristan stops. I convince him that we should eat lunch before going, and in strained silence we pick berries from a few bushes. I eat slowly, dreading the end of the sweet meal even more than I would the end of a summer vacation.

When it's time to close my eyes and ride the interplane, I feel as though I'm falling back into the arms of the Great Alula, as though she's cradling me in the softness of her light wings. The vibration feels so good I want it to last forever. I want to float, to fly forever. Never again to worry or doubt or fear. Just to *be*.

But I know that the relief of a weekend always leads to the shock of a Monday; and the bliss of a daydream, to the jolt of real life. And so it is now, when much sooner than I'd like, the comforting darkness gives way to a faint light, to the smell of moisture and the feel of a fine mist spray. For a moment I think I'm back on the human plane, standing at the bus stop on one of those mist-spray mornings when the sky can't decide whether or not to rain and the kids can't decide whether to put their umbrellas up and risk looking uncool or keep them closed and risk getting wet.

Then I look around.

And notice there is no mist. No bus stop.

Instead, I find myself inside a huge, dome-shaped . . . something. It certainly isn't a building, whatever it is: the walls that curve around me seem too much like slabs of clear jelly. But *are* they even walls? It looks like I could stick my leg through one of them as easily as I'd poke a finger in a bowl full of gelatin.

"Tristan! Welcome," says a voice stranger than any I've ever heard. I can't tell if it's male or female, but it sounds exactly like the voice running water would have if it could speak.

"Thanks. I'm glad to be back," says another fluid voice.

Recognizing the second as Tristan's—without its masculine tinge—I catch sight of a bright light to my left. No, not just light: a shapeless mass, part water, part light, that shines with a greenish color the same shade as Tristan's glow. Right away, I know it's Tristan. Him, yet not him.

"Where's the Alula? Have you brought her with you?" This fluid voice draws my attention to a dozen more masses of glowing water-light. They are all gliding toward us as fast as a group of spilled drinks running from their containers.

"I thought I did," says Tristan, puzzled. "I'm sure I did!" Then, more gently: "Hesper? Are you there?"

I step forward but feel no jelly-like floor against the bottoms of my feet. Looking down, I see nothing but the barren soil beneath the clear floor. No feet. No body. Nothing.

Unlike in my out-of-body dream, this time when I want to scream, I can. And I do.

16

Illume

"Hesper, where are you?" I hear Tristan cry. "What's wrong?"

"Tristan, I can't see myself. I'm . . . nothing!" My voice sounds faint and funny, but it's a wonder I can talk at all, for I have no tongue, no mouth.

"Okay, don't panic. Where are you?"

"Right beside you," I say to the green water-light.

Though the glowing form has no head to turn, no eyes to see, I could swear it does turn, it does see. "Wow," Tristan says. "You're completely invisible."

"What's happened to me, Tristan?"

"I don't know, Hesper."

"Well, what's happened to you?"

This question sends a ripple through the other water-lights, followed by a sound that reminds me of a stream rushing down its pebble-paved path. I'm not sure, but I think it's laughter. I think they're laughing at me.

Tristan answers, "This is my illume."

"Your what?"

"My illume."

"What's that?"

More ripples, more laughter.

"The essence without the body," explains Tristan. "The content without the container. The part of me that never dies." He pauses. Uneasily: "I don't know why I can't see your illume."

An orange water-light slides forward. "Tristan, you know very well that voids don't have illumes."

"She's not a void!" Tristan snaps.

"She said it herself," persists the orange. "She's 'nothing.'"

"We don't know that for sure," cuts in a reddish Dyaphinee. "Not until Aeon returns do we know anything for sure."

"Why should we wait until Aeon returns? Can't we think for ourselves?" spouts the voice of a yellow water-light splotched brown in several places. All the other Dyaphinees have patches here and there where their light dims and their fluid grows murky, but the patches on this one are strikingly bigger, darker. Like scum on the surface of a pond. "Aeon will take forever praying to the Eternal One," the yellow continues. "Why should we wait when it's obvious these beings are all voids? They're unworthy of hearing the message we bring them. They're so ignorant they actually believe us to be the problem instead of the cure!" As it speaks, a handful of new water-lights—all of them just as noticeably splotched—glide over and gather around it.

"We are neither the problem *nor* the cure," corrects Tristan.

"What do you mean?" I ask.

"Just don't pay any attention to him, Hesper," says Tristan. "When Aeon comes back, he'll explain everything."

The yellow one slides closer to Tristan. "You, my friend, have spent far too much time among the aliens."

Tristan retorts, "Whatever time *you* spent was too much, since it turned your compassion into pride."

The yellow laughs. "Why, I believe you have feelings for this alien. Beware: they rob you of your good judgment." He turns back to the other water-lights. "See—Tristan no longer knows the difference between an illume and a void!"

"That's not true!" is Tristan's angry reply. "After all, we can hear her. What are we hearing if it isn't her illume?"

The yellow one slides menacingly closer. "Voids have many ways of tricking you into thinking they aren't empty. But the fact is, we can't *see* her." His voice lowers to a gurgle. "Tell me: what does this void look like on the other planes? Does it look lovely in its physical shell? It must to have deceived you so."

"Hey!" I shout, too insulted to remember how terrified I am. "You may not be able to see me, but that doesn't mean I'm not here. So if you've got something to say about me, you can just say it to my face—I mean, my . . . um. . . ." I sigh. "You can just say it to me!"

When the splotched water-light turns and ripple-laughs at me, I see in a flash what it might look like in human form. Like one of those bullies at school with scornful smiles uglier even than frowns. "Why should I talk to a void?"

Again, my vexation chases the fear away. "Who are you to judge what I am?"

"All right, then prove to us you have an illume. Prove to us you deserve to hear our message."

I can't help but laugh at his childish demand, even though it does scare me. "You act like an illume is a cell you can stain with iodine in science class. I don't think you know any more about illumes than I do."

At this, a curious thing happens. The blotches on the Dyaphinee swirl and darken like thunderclouds brooding against a yellow sky. "I *have* an illume!" he spouts. "And I know enough about them to say this: if you had an illume, it would be visible, just like the rest of ours!"

No sooner has he finished shouting when all the Dyaphinees start talking in one great rush of fluid voices—one crashing waterfall of shouting and arguing and agreeing and disagreeing. I think I hear Tristan's voice among them, but I can't understand what he says. I can't understand what any of them say, these talking, glowing blobs of rainbow. I can only turn inside and ask:

How do I know for sure I have an illume? How do I know it?

I don't. I just know that without an inner life—a quiet self perched deep inside me, waiting to fly on as soon as my physical wings turn to dust—everything I do, everything I feel, everything I am in this life seems a waste. Without it, why laugh? Why cry? Why hope, dream, love? Wouldn't it all be pointless?

I look down at the jelly-like floor, straining in vain to see some sign of myself. Again, nothing. I try to accept the bleak conclusion that I am empty. That when I die, no part of me will live on. That I'll simply cease to be. Forever. I feel like I'm caught in one of those nightmares where, no matter how fast you run, you go nowhere; no matter how much you struggle to move forward, you stay just as stuck—and just as maddened by the uselessness of it all.

But something inside me says: No.

Something inside won't let me despair. Something lifts me up even as I start to fall.

It begins with a tremble, a flutter that spreads into a vibration, a now-familiar lightness more extraordinary than anything I've ever felt—yet at the same time, as natural as breathing. And in a lightning-tingle of awareness, a sense of remembrance I cannot place, I know. I know I'm not empty, and it doesn't matter who else does or doesn't think so. I know it because I feel it. And that's all that matters.

I look up at the sky, at the stars slightly distorted by the clear gelatin ceiling. I have no lips, but I smile; no arms, but I lift them high—high above the head I also don't have.

I could fly there, I think. *I could fly there—right now!*

And then, all at once, every single fluid voice falls silent.

"Aeon!" I hear someone say. "We didn't think . . . we didn't expect. . . ."

I look back down. There, in the doorless oval opening to the jelly-dome, is the most radiant water-light of all.

17

Aeon

The bluest blue and the brightest bright.

The ocean and the sun together as one.

This is the being they call Aeon. This is the illume I see—an illume that, no doubt, I could not behold with my physical eyes. For the light would probably blind them.

At first I think the beautiful Dyaphinee has no brown splotches at all. But as he glides toward us, I notice they are there, only so small, so faint that the light still shines through them. When at last he speaks, I get an urge to laugh. There's nothing amusing about his voice or his words, yet how I want to laugh!

"Welcome, Tristan," Aeon says. Like the others, his liquid voice sounds neither male nor female. But I remember Tristan describing him as an old Mantaur, so I immediately see him as male, though I somehow sense he has no gender. At least not in this form.

To my surprise, Aeon turns in my direction. "Welcome, Hesper. Please forgive my brothers and sisters for their rudeness. I've been gone but a short while, and already some have lost faith."

"You can see me?" My voice carries my excitement.

"No, but I feel the presence of your illume."

"You can?" I say, laughing. Not funny-laughter but deep inside joy-laughter. "I can feel it, too."

"Good. You're overcoming your fear."

Once again, I glance down at where my feet should be. "Can you feel the presence of my body, too? Or did I leave it behind on the other plane?"

"The body and the illume can't be permanently separated until death," Aeon explains. "Your body is there with you but imperceptible, just as your illume is imperceptible on the other planes."

The yellow water-light makes a sound like a brook running over gravel; it reminds me of a throat being cleared. "But why would her illume be imperceptible on this plane, too?" he asks, his voice more subdued than before. "This is the plane where outer forms are not sensed, where the only shape you take is the shape of your illume; the only color, the color of your illume. If this being had an illume, we would see it, wouldn't we?"

Aeon answers, "When have you seen the Eternal One?"

"But this is different," insists the yellow.

"How so?" asks Aeon. "We don't know everything about the Eternal One, and we don't know everything about the beings of this planet. Obviously, they are unlike us: they take on forms unlike ours."

"That's exactly my point," says the yellow. "The beings on the human plane do things that stain far worse than the things we do. Yet it doesn't show on their forms. Neither they nor any others see the dark blotch of offense upon them. Surely they must be voids. They have no illumes to stain."

"Not so, brother. The blotch of offense does indeed stain them—and just as deeply as it stains us. But their tainted illumes are hidden inside the disguise of bodies you can't see through. Attractive, well-groomed on the outside, these beings can be badly stained on the inside. But most don't know it. And so they continue doing those things in their outer lives

that stain the inner lives they have no awareness of." Aeon turns to me again. "Hesper,
this is why the Eternal One sent us to your
planet. To remind the humans of this inner
life."

"That's it?" I ask, almost disappointed.
"That's the message?"

I think about the staggering distance they
must have traveled from their planet to bring
this message. All that to say something so
simple, so obvious. Or is it? It's like hearing
someone from halfway around the globe say,
"Hey, I just dropped by to remind you you've
got lungs." It's like realizing with a jolt that,
though you breathe all the time, you hardly
ever think about your lungs.

"But . . . the planes," I say. "They're
blending together, you know. Because you're
here."

"You see!" exclaims the yellow. "I told
you! They're so ignorant they think—"

"Please!" Aeon shouts. And more quietly:
"It's not for you to judge."

The splotches on the yellow water-light
swirl and darken once again. "Is no one but
you allowed to judge? You have no right,
Aeon, to criticize my judgment when it's

yours that falls short. I can indeed judge for myself—and I will from now on! *You* are not the Eternal One." He glides swiftly to the oval opening. "Who else here finds fault in *Aeon's* judgment?" The handful of splotched water-lights who surrounded him before as he argued with Tristan now float over and follow him as he leaves. "Beware, void!" he yells from outside. The walls of the jelly dome distort his dark patches, making them seem bigger. "You can't help us; you can only put yourself in greater danger!"

I watch uneasily as he and his followers glide away along the barren, pock-marked ground. More water-lights stay than leave, though, and those who remain murmur their shock.

"Please forgive him, Hesper," Aeon says. "He hasn't always been that way." He sighs a light water-sigh. "Tristan told us you hear voices when you're on the Alula plane. Sad voices from nowhere."

"Yes." It makes me feel sort of sad, just thinking about them. "I hear them at night, mostly."

"Those voices are the reason the planes are blending," says Aeon.

"What do you mean?"

Aeon pauses, and as he does, I think I start to hear the sad voices calling: faintly, like the first trickles of rain falling somewhere far away. "Hesper, listen to the voices, and you'll know what I mean. For they have been telling you all along."

"But I can't understand what they say."

"Yes, you can. Listen with the ears you know you have, though neither you nor we can see them. Look with the eyes you know to be there, though you can't even blink them. Feel with the part that fills you up with lightness the moment you think, 'I'm empty.' "

The joy in Aeon's voice makes the voices sound all the more mournful when he stops speaking, leaving only their growing cries in my ears. I try to do as he says, but it isn't until I stop trying—until I let go—that I actually begin to understand.

The first word I understand is "help."

It isn't just the word itself I understand. It's where it comes from, what it feels like. It comes from the human plane, and it feels like a horrible numbness.

"Help," it whispers. "I'm depressed, unloved, alone." At the same time, an image flashes before me: a picture of the voice. It's a teenage girl pacing around with a bottle of pills in her fist, and seeing her, I think, *That poor girl is paralyzed.*

"I search for comfort in the dark but only find more darkness." I see the boy with the stained shirt in the courtyard, buying drugs from a friend. His wild eyes are lit up by a false light.

"I've lost myself and don't know what to look for." I see many people, young and old, all busy on the outside, all still as stagnant ponds on the inside. Paralyzed.

"I can't feel for people; they are just things to be used." I see a figure following someone down a dim street, stalking like a Mantaur hunting his prey.

"There's no God to punish me, and nothing I do matters." I see the face of a killer, the victim reflected, trapped and terror-stricken, in the killer's vacant eyes. The horror seeps down in me, headache-heavy, then wrenches up through me in a sob not my own, yet more my own than I can bear.

I don't let myself hear or see any more.

Focusing on Aeon again, I allow the voices, the pictures—everything—to fade back into their unintelligible state. "So all along," I whisper, almost too drained to feel amazed, "it's been the plane's own beings causing the blending?"

"Yes," says Aeon.

"But it's not all of them. And most of the troubled ones aren't bad." I mention the depressed girl and the boy in the courtyard. "They're just weighed down by the rotten parts of life. I've felt that way, too. All they need is hope."

"I agree. Those are the ones who can be reached first, who can lift the plane's awareness back up. But they need our message."

I find myself remembering the stories of the Bible—how again and again people lost hope and prophets were sent to restore it. "But the prophets in the old days . . . they were all human beings who belonged to the plane—or at least to this planet. Why did the Eternal One send aliens this time?"

"Please don't compare us to your prophets. Where we come from, we're considered very ordinary."

"But you're not full of fear," I say, thinking of myself.

"We had to be brave to make the journey

here," Aeon concedes.

"But why didn't beings from another plane on *this* planet bring the message?"

"Because if you scrape your left knee, you don't tear the skin off your right knee and cover the scrape with it. You use something outside your body—a drop of medicine, a bandage—to heal it. This planet's other planes are like the right knee. Their beings should stay on their own planes, so as not to further disrupt the balance. But the Council of the Alulas has been speeding up the imbalance by Sending to the human plane Alulas who don't have the right awareness for that plane."

"Speeding up?" I cry. The simultaneous craziness and logic of this revelation makes me reel. "But they're trying to stop the blend-ing!"

"Good intentions can be dangerous when you think you know more than you do," Aeon says. "And to make matters worse, the Alulas are trying to figure out how to ride the inter-plane without forgetting. Because of this Alula threat, most of us have left the human plane, where we were peacefully spreading our mes-sage, to hide here on this plane. For the Alulas could kill us on the human plane, where our bodies are vulnerable and weapons can be used."

I look over at the green illume. Though I know my friend can't see me, I could swear he turns and looks back at me, just the way he always would. "So how can I help?" I hear myself ask—before I even decide to ask it.

"We'd be grateful," says Aeon, "if you would tell the Alulas what I've told you: that we are here to help halt the blending, not cause it. Ease their fearful minds so they stop hastening the blending. Then we can return to the human plane, spread our message in safety, and be on our way home."

My mind can't accept the possibility of Tristan being on his way to any other home but his cave, and especially not to some unknown planet utterly unreachable by me. So I push Aeon's last words aside and focus instead on his request.

"But what if the Council members don't believe me?" I ask. "I know they'd believe you. The way you speak, the joy in your voice . . . they couldn't help but believe you."

"It doesn't matter how loud your voice is when you speak to a deaf man: he still cannot hear you. Look at my own group. Some be-

lieve me and some don't. Whether I tell the
Alulas or you do, it's still up to them to believe. And right now the Alulas are ready to
kill aliens, not listen to them."

The truth in his words makes me ashamed
for being an Alula.

"Hesper, I've given you something you
can now pass on to the Alulas: the ability to
understand with your illume what the sad
voices say. This is how you can tell them our
message. By passing on to them the ability to
understand the voices."

"But they can't even *hear* the voices," I
say. "How am I supposed to make them understand them?"

"You don't need to 'make' them understand anything. With your presence, you'll
help them hear, just as I with my presence
have helped you hear. *Truly* hear. But they
must come to understand for themselves."

"Oh." How easy . . . and how hard. But
how wonderful if the Alulas can understand!
The possibility infuses me with hope, but then
the voices drift in again with all their gloom,
and I teeter between joy and despair like a kite
torn between the upward urging of the wind
and the downward yanking of the string. "All

right," I say. "I'll be honored to do it."

The green illume beside me glides closer. "I'll come with you."

"You're no longer safe there, Tristan," warns Aeon.

"Neither is Hesper," he says. "I have to go with her."

His words, I think, inspire the Dyaphinees' version of the Alulas' knowing glances.

A soft ripple runs through Aeon: a smile. "Thank you. Both of you."

Once outside the jelly dome, Tristan and I continue until, again, we are surrounded on all sides by wide open space.

Tristan stops and asks, "Hesper, are you with me?"

"Yes."

"Are you ready?"

I look behind me, almost to make sure the jelly dome is still there—or even was there in the first place. And yes, it is and was, this clear gelatin mold that from here reminds me of an upside-down glass serving bowl. And yes, they are and were, these colorful water-lights that, from inside the see-through bowl, bob and glow like caught fireflies.

I turn back to Tristan. Part of me is afraid

for him, but another part is terribly glad I don't have to return without him.

"Yes," I say, "I'm ready."

18

Enchantment

The first thing I notice when we reach the Alula plane is how uncomfortable it feels to be inside a body again. It's almost like putting clothes on in the morning—like feeling the roughness of the tag against the back of my neck, the tightness of the belt around my waist. Like that, only different. On the barren plain I was free. Free from worrying: How do I look? What should I do with my wings? Should I sit or stand? Now, as the physical sensations come back, I feel cramped and awkward; trapped inside my own familiar limbs.

This makes it all the more startling when, suddenly, a hand touches my wing. Without thinking, I jump.

"You're afraid of me still," Tristan says, sadly turning away.

"No, it's not that," I say. "It's just that . . . it feels weird."

He nods. "I know."

I look into his eyes. At the illume captured there. "Tristan, did all that really happen? That was amazing."

His eyes look back into mine. Searching; as always, reaching. "Do you forgive me?"

"For what?" I ask.

He shrugs. "For being an alien."

"Nothing to forgive there. But I do forgive you for not telling me sooner."

"So you trust me again?"

I think for a moment. "I trust Aeon." I smile apologetically. "I should have known to trust you, too."

We start for the cave, and Tristan trots ahead, then hurries back, beaming down at his hooves. "Look! My legs improved again."

His legs do appear less scrawny and more muscular. "That's great! I'm so glad, Tris." I spread my wings and see no sign of my arms returning.

"I hoped for it," he says, "but I left it up to the Eternal One. I guess I was wrong about the sacrifice being permanent."

"But my damage is the same."

"Maybe because you haven't sacrificed your body as many times." Tristan gazes at my outstretched wings as he speaks, admiring them, making my feathers feel as sensitive as if it were him, instead of the breeze, caressing them. But he's not a boy and I'm not quite a girl, and we're not strolling home from a high school dance. I fold my wings.

We walk in silence, watching the stars and—out of the corners of our eyes—each other. The night is cool and gentle and enchanted. So enchanted that dreams could be reality, and reality just as distant as the most far-fetched dreams. The air holds its breath as the sad voices cry out, and this time I answer them with an inward prayer.

"Tristan? The way you looked on the barren plane . . . was it your true form? I mean, the way you'd look on your planet?"

"No, that was my illume-form. On my planet, I would have a body, but it wouldn't be anything like this one." He gestures down at his half-human, half-horse's body. "And it would be see-through, so you could see my illume, with all its stains."

I think of Mom's theory about souls born from the same star. It's a nice notion, but I don't think it explains the affinity between Tristan and me. How can you come from the same star when you aren't even from the same *planet,* when your very illumes seem to be made of different stuff? It still hurts, to know how foreign Tristan truly is to me, yet how dear. Glancing over at his bright silhouette, I try to imagine what it would be like to see everyone's insides. Everyone's heart beating, blood pulsating, bones and joints working. Somehow, this doesn't seem nearly as troubling as the prospect of reading people's illumes just by looking at them. Would I want everyone to see straight into my illume? Would I want to see into everyone else's? The concept gives a world of new meaning to the expression "seeing right through you." And to the term "honesty." People would have to tell the truth because they couldn't hide anything anyway. And there would be no more emphasis on outer beauty. Instead, society might become obsessed with inner beauty—literally. But then again, people wouldn't so easily forget about their illumes like they do now . . . .

"Tristan, why do humans keep needing reminders of their illumes?"

"Well, Aeon says it's because they're so clever."

I frown. "But it's good to be clever."

"True. Unless you're too clever to figure out the simplest thing."

"What?"

"Well, take a look at Aeon," he says. "Aeon's very clever. He helped design that spaceship we were just in. So you might say he's like one of those brilliant scientists they have on the human plane. Right?"

"I guess so." I try to picture the jelly dome in my mind. Nothing but see-through gelatin. Who would have thought it was a spaceship?

Tristan continues, "Aeon also knows when *not* to be clever."

"You mean he knows that some things aren't meant to be thought about."

"Exactly," says Tristan. "The trick is knowing when it's right to use your mind and when it's wrong to. If you don't know this, an intelligent mind can be a dangerous thing."

I nod. "Yeah, well, all I have to say is—I sure wish that yellow Dyaphinee were a lot stupider!"

Tristan laughs. "Me, too!"

I laugh along—laughter I've been wanting to let out ever since I first heard Aeon speak. When we reach the cave entrance, I linger there, not only because I don't want to face the

Council yet, but because I don't want to leave
Tristan yet.

He looks like he doesn't want me to leave
either, and his wistful words confirm it: "I
wish you could stay for a while, like in the old
days." But the feeling between us is not quite
like the old days, for as he speaks he gazes
from my eyes to my lips and back again, like
a date who doesn't know how to ask for a
good-night kiss. I find myself drawn to his lips
as well, which hold the same unearthly beauty
as the rest of him.

"You know, Tris, on the human plane . . .
I missed you. Even though I couldn't remember."

His lips break into a slow grin. "Good," he
says softly.

I smile back at him, and for a moment, it
feels like we've always been close; like we
were never really so distant, never really so
different. Like we've always been just as we
are—two beings standing together, peering in
quiet wonder at one another.

"You must rather be on your planet." I
don't know why I blurt this out, except that
the joy of our closeness draws out my aver-
sion to our being apart, and my dismay at Ae-

on's mention of the aliens heading home.

"I'd rather be with you," he says with a sincerity that both exhilarates and pains me.

"But your planet . . . it's not falling apart, not dangerous, like mine."

"I like danger, remember?" He tries to say it in a joking way, but I can see in his face that he has more respect for danger than he used to.

"If the planes go back to normal, I hope you won't have to leave," I say pensively.

He takes his time answering, as though he can't bear to tell the truth, just as I can't bear to hear it. "Me, too, but it's up to Aeon. We came here as a bandage, to help heal the wound and be on our way. Aeon thinks the planes might get disrupted all over again if we stay past the point we're needed."

Aeon's logic would make perfect sense if only I didn't have a heart to be pierced by it. Again, the possibility of Tristan returning to his planet is too upsetting for me to contemplate, so I force myself to face the problem at hand.

I sigh. "I'd better go see the Council."

Tristan's expression is tender as he steps closer and lifts his hand to touch my hair. In the old days he would have picked some fuzz out of it or teased me about its tangles; now, he gently strokes it. His palm barely brushes my cheek, but I can feel it all through me, just as if he wraps his arms around me and holds me.

"I'll wait here. Be careful, Hess."

"You, too, Tris."

19

Another Friend

I know I should feel worried; I know I should be scared. But as I fly to the Council's skymount, all I feel is an inner peace, a strange calmness.

Nitza is waiting for me at the same entrance to the interior. "The Council is assembled," is her terse greeting.

"Already?" I ask.

"We've been watching closely for your return."

Once again she leads me down the stairway and the tunnelway to the Council room. There, two rows of lined faces stare up at me even more anxiously than before.

"Thank you, Nitza. You may go home for the night."

Nitza exits grudgingly, the disappointment plain on her face.

I take my seat, meeting the Council Wing's questioning glance with an involuntary smile. She returns it—warily.

"My child, does this mean good news?"

"Well . . . yes, sort of."

"Then you have found a way to kill the aliens?"

I hesitate. "Well . . . no."

Her face falls. All around the table, expressions transform from hopeful to hopeless like lights controlled by the same switch.

"Have you not visited the barren plane?" asks one Alula.

"Have you not discovered the Boytaur's true identity?"

"And his deceit?" hisses another.

"I've discovered a lot more than that." Every part of me but my voice seems to shake as I explain about Aeon and the other Dyaphinees, about the simple message they traveled so far to bring, about the real reason the planes are blending. "All this you can feel for yourselves to be true," I say. "Just come to the surface with me and listen to the sad voices like I did. Aeon said you'll be able to hear them now."

I get up, walk confidently to the wide, closed door. But I'm followed only by reluctant eyes.

"There's nothing to be afraid of," I try to reassure them, realizing for once what it must feel like to be in Tristan's hooves. "Trust me: I'm telling the truth."

I open the door—just in time to see someone jump to the side in a blur of black hair and light brown wings.

"Nitza!" shouts Moira.

Nitza steps guiltily back into the doorway opening.

The Council Wing stands. "You know you are not to listen in on the business of this Council. You have not yet earned that privilege."

Nitza stares down at the floor, ashamed.

"You should be home!" chides Moira.

The Council Wing looks from me to Nitza. She sighs. "Since you are here, you might as well come with us to the surface. We may have another task for you after all."

Nitza appears almost as excited as I feel as the Alulas rise to go.

On the way to the surface, I try to remember everything Aeon told me—all that about listening with the ears you have but can't see you have. The version I deliver doesn't sound nearly as eloquent as Aeon's, but the Council members still understand it with ease. After all, these Alulas are used to talking about whole *planes* we have but can't see we have.

"So if you could let go the way you do before Sendings. . . ." I finish feebly once we reach the surface. Already I have to talk over the forlorn whispers of the voices.

The Alulas stand in a circle and close their eyes. I hate to have to hear the voices again—to feel so keenly their empty despair—but I know I must if I want to help.

I can tell the Alulas feel the despair when they echo the voices' cries with horrified gasps of their own. And when the Council Wing chases the cries back into their unintelligible state with a loud, angry: "Enough!"

All eyes pop open and look to the Council Wing. The Council Wing looks to me.

"Hesper, we have heard the voices with you. Now we will hear them with*out* you and feel for ourselves if they are what you claim them to be."

She gestures to Nitza. Nitza breaks from the circle and approaches her for instructions, her face part disturbed, part dazed with revelation. My heart thumps. Can it be that Nitza understands?

"Take her below. . . ." the Council Wing tells Nitza. I don't catch the rest of her instructions because the Council members surround me and ask questions about the aliens, staring suspiciously at me.

I bombard Nitza with questions of my own on our way down the stairs to the interior.

"Could you tell where the voices came from?" I keep asking the back of her head while I follow her. "Could you tell it was the human plane?"

Only once does she turn as if to answer, and then I can see the conflict in her thoughtful eyes. But the look on her face is the only answer she gives me because she doesn't say anything. She doesn't turn around again until we reach the waiting room across the hall from the Council room, and by this time her face has gone blank.

She opens the door. "Wait in here."

Grudgingly I walk in, take a seat, and assume she'll leave. But she doesn't. She starts to, then stops in the doorway with her back to me and her head tilted slightly to the side. I fix my gaze on the wooden shelves stacked with reading tablets, thinking she'll be gone by the time I look back at the doorway.

Still, she does not leave. Instead, she turns and stares at me in that striking way of hers, her wide eyes fascinated. "What's it like," she asks shyly, "having a friend like that? Having someone to share your time and your thoughts with?"

I don't answer right away. I'm too used to hearing her say things like "Follow me" and "The Council is assembled" not to be taken aback by such an unexpected question. "Well, um . . ." I begin, "I guess it's sort of like the difference between flying and bounce-flying. When you fly alone, you get tired easily and you can't go very far or very high. But when you fly with someone else—I mean, bounce-fly—you don't get so tired and you fly farther and higher."

She nods in understanding, then frowns and shakes her head. "But friends can leave. And it's harder to fly alone again once you get used to bounce-flying."

I'm tempted to agree. The threat of the aliens' departure is indeed enough to make me want to distance myself from Tristan emotionally—if only I could. But it isn't enough to make me regret being close to him. Nitza's argument for isolation makes me think of how my life was before I made friends with Tristan. How lonely I felt. And, despite that loneliness, how quick I was to thwart all potential friendships with other Alulas.

"Nitza, don't you have any friends?"

"I'm very busy," she says defensively. "There's always much to learn, much work to do for the Council." She holds her head a little higher. "I'll be a Council member someday."

Delicately, I say, "And when that time comes, who will be glad for you? Who will care?"

She says nothing. We both awkwardly turn our attention to the shelves stacked with reading tablets. When she does finally speak, it isn't to answer, but to question again. "Is it scary being friends with an alien?"

I smile at the similarity between us. "It shouldn't be."

"The Council suspects you're more than friends," she says, her voice low and confidential. "They suspect you're in love. They're afraid of that. Afraid for us, afraid for you."

My heart jumps like a moth flying up in a frenzy when someone steps near the blade of grass where it hides. "What!" I exclaim. "He's an *alien*. We can't be anything but friends. It's impossible!" I say, more to myself than to her. "I can't believe the Council would think . . . !" I feel just as indignant—and just as embarrassed—as I would if she were Marcie teasing me about liking the cute new boy at school.

For the first time since I've known her, Nitza smiles. A small knowing smile. Just enough for me to notice that her front teeth are a little crooked. "I think it would be nice to have a friend."

Then before I even get a chance to reply, she turns and leaves, closing the door firmly behind her. I spend the rest of my waiting time sitting there in silence, nervous about the Council's decision, glad about my conversation with Nitza, but upset over what Nitza said about Tristan. *Why* does everybody have to accuse me of pining for Tristan? It only draws to the surface all the feelings I don't want to deal with.

This time when Nitza comes to inform me that the Council is ready, her voice isn't quite so impersonal and her lips are curved into a vague, shy smile.

But the faces of the Council members as they greet me in the Council room are not soft with smiles, vague or otherwise.

"My child," begins the Council Wing in a solemn tone, "we have listened to these voices impartially. We have heard their calls for help. We have seen their pitiful state. But we have not felt them to originate from the human plane."

I glance around the table in disbelief, anxious for someone—anyone—to disagree. But the eyes that watch me are all the same: uncertain, frightened, like children's eyes in old faces. I catch my breath, afraid again—and hating the familiar feel of it.

The Council Wing looks away. "This Aeon is terribly wrong. These are not the cries of humans who have lost awareness. They are the future cries of Alulas and Mantaurs being crushed in the interplanar blending to come." She glares at me. "The blending these aliens are causing!"

My jaw drops. "What! Alulas and Mantaurs? How . . . ?"

"Hesper," says Moira, "we knew your feelings for the Boytaur made you distrust us. But we thought that after you discovered his true identity and traveled to the barren plane, you would realize how to carry out your great duty and help us. But instead, it seems your feelings for the Boytaur have hindered you from hearing the voices objectively. You say the voices come from the human plane. Why? Because you do not want to believe your friend would trick you . . . again."

No! I want to scream. I felt it! It wasn't because of Tristan. I felt it!

"Think, my child," the Council Wing urges. "Use your brain, not your emotions. If what you say were true, we would be the first to help these aliens stop the blending. But the evidence is all against the aliens, no matter what words this Aeon used to charm you. And of all the Alulas to befriend, the Boytaur chose you: the only one with the ability to identify the aliens by their glows and therefore destroy them, saving two planes from blending. Do you call that chance? No, my child. He knew exactly what he was doing when he befriended you."

I rise on shaking feet. "No! Tristan didn't plan to become friends with me. He didn't even know he was one of the Dyaphinees back then. And why would he teach me their secret—how to ride the interplane without forgetting—if he knew I could use it to destroy them?"

Moira says, "He took a big chance there. And it looks as though it paid off."

"No," corrects the Council Wing. "He *thinks* it paid off." She pushes away a stray wisp of silver hair and looks me squarely in the eyes. "But this friendship he so strategically made will yet be the undoing of his kind."

I step back, alarmed by her odd likeness to my algebra teacher just before he announces one of his dreaded pop quizzes. Then the Council Wing rises to her feet, and I find myself longing for my teacher, for the minor threat of a little pop quiz.

"Yes, my child," the Council Wing says. "You will save the planes yet. The Mantaurs can see the alien glow, but they cannot ride the interplane. We Alulas can ride the interplane, but we cannot see this characteristic glow. Only you can do both. You will teach us how to ride the interplane without forgetting. Then you will travel to each plane with us. One by one, you will identify the alien messengers by their glows. And we will kill them—every one of them—before they kill our plane."

"Never!" I whisper, backing away.

The Council Wing steps forward. The

lamplight casts a shadow across her face, splotching it. "I wonder if the Boytaur knows his life depends on your cooperation." She pauses, and I feel the panic surfacing against my will in my eyes. "I wonder: does he know, sitting and waiting in his cave?"

Silence. Then, before I even think to do it, I'm lunging for the door, swatting frantically the wings that lash at me along the way. Swatting—and screaming—when they grab my wing from behind. Screaming—and kicking—when they grab hold of my wing and yank.

The door flies open.

"Nitza, no!" screeches the Council Wing.

Nitza stares. "I-I heard—"

"Stop her!"

For a second I see Nitza's figure in the doorway, tentatively blocking my way. Then she blurs to the side and I run.

20

Flight

I am a tornado—
A swirl of emotions
A flurry of wings
A frantic mass of charged nerves,
Short breaths, shaking limbs: panic.
Yet somewhere inside—
Deep inside, at the silent center of me—
Calm.
Still calm.

"Tristan!" I scream before my feet even hit the resilient ground and start their race to the cave. "Tristan, we've gotta go! Hurry!"

He must be listening for me because he comes galloping out while I'm still some distance away. He slows down enough for me to climb onto his back and wrap my wings around his waist—a little too tightly, because I'm so relieved to see him. And because I'm afraid I'll fall off without hands to grip hold the way they usually would.

"Where to?" he calls over his shoulder as he speeds up.

"Another plane! Any plane!"

Where else? I think wildly. *Where else?*

There is nowhere else. Nowhere to run but an endless stretch of moss-covered hills with few trees. Nowhere to hide but the deserted caves of Mantaurs—probably the first places the Council will think to look for us. Nowhere to go but another place at the same place. Nothing to do but stay away from this plane— this beautiful and awful plane of childhood and sad voices and fear and bounce-flying and sneaking off to see Tristan—forever. Stay away like a Sent Alula. Like all the Sent Alulas, stay away.

"This is wide open enough, isn't it?" I ask, my voice tense with urgency. "Come on— let's just *go!*"

Tristan slows to a stop, and I close my eyes, try to take the panic and impatience and push it all away. Relax. Sigh. Trust in the Great Alula, in God, in the Eternal One. In whatever it is that is all of these and none; in what is too wide, too all-encompassing, too unimaginable to be one beautiful Alula with wings outstretched. Or one kindly old man with beard long and flowing. Or even one biggest, brightest water-light you can think of. Because you can't *think of*—you can only trust and open up and love and feel. . . .

"Too late!"

It's Tristan's voice that jerks me out of my quiet state, I know. But it sounds too frightened to be his. No, it can't be.

It is his voice: awakening my ears and eyes to the sound of wings beating and male voices yelling; the sight of hoofed, winged figures—too many of them to count—dropping down like bombs out of the serene, dark sky. Then Tristan's voice yelling, "Hold on!" and his arms pulling me forward against his back and his hooves pounding the soft earth harder than I've ever known. Pounding, racing—where? Where to run? Where to hide?

There is nowhere. Nowhere! Oh, Great Alula—oh, God!—there is nowhere.

I press my cheek against Tristan's shoulder, smell the familiar scent of him. Of him sweating. Or is it me sweating? I can feel his muscles straining, hear his breath growing pained and heavy. How long can his legs hold out? How long can we run before the stampede of hooves catches up with us? I think we pass one of the stakes that mark the road by the school, but I can't tell for certain. I can't even tell where we are anymore. The bottoms of my bare feet prickle with panic, with nerve endings tensed and knotting up on themselves.

"No!"

Tristan swerves and turns sharply as another group of Alulas-astride-Mantaurs gallops straight for us. I'm so shocked by Tristan's outcry—almost more than I am by the new danger—that I nearly forget to hold on. Tristan can't be afraid. He isn't supposed to be. He can't!

But the other Mantaurs can, and the Alulas, too, because all at once they are—screaming and yelling out their fear. Insanely, as if they've forgotten they're the chasers instead of the chased. But they *are* the chased, for out of nowhere comes a strange skidding sound— too loud to be the skidding of a Mantaur's hooves, too mechanical even to belong to this plane. A kind of out-of-place skidding that I haven't heard since . . .

Since Tristan crossed the street without looking on the way to the deserted field.

With a gasp, I glance back, see the harsh brightness of headlights filtering through the fleeing crowd, the lit-up terror on the faces of Alulas and Mantaurs as they swerve to the side, fly up, or fall at the wheels of a great metal monster. A car. It knocks through them like a bowling ball through pins.

We are the last pin. It comes so close to ramming into us that for an instant I can see the faces inside the windshield as they stare out at me, mouths gaping, eyes wide, aghast.

And then the faces are gone. Just like that: gone. As fast as sad voices dropping back into nothingness, though I can't really call it nothingness anymore.

I let out my breath and turn around—just in time to glimpse the second car right before it sideswipes us.

It happens so suddenly: one moment I'm crouched forward on Tristan's back, wings clasped around him, and the next moment I'm lying on the ground smelling the faintly nauseating smell of car exhaust and listening to the sound of someone groaning.

Tristan groaning.

I reach out for him with my wing. "Tris!"

His eyes open wearily, close again. "Fly!"

he commands.

All around us hooves are pounding, wings flapping, voices shouting out, some in triumph over us, some in anger and despair over the car's victims. Mantaurs, Alulas: closing in from every side.

"Fly!" His voice is barely a whisper above the mob now; his eyes don't open again.

All I can think of is what Aeon said about Tristan not being safe, about the Alulas being ready to kill aliens. I lunge for Tristan, spreading my wings over as much of his body as I can—a weak shield, but the only one I have. His back legs feel wet and sticky with blood, but the rise and fall of his breathing assures me he isn't dead. It is this—his breathing, his life—that I hold onto in the charged seconds before they reach us and my head is thumped painfully from behind, sending my mind floating, sighing: calm.

21

No Escape

"Hess, wake up!"

No. I don't want to. My head hurts. I can't.

"Hess, please."

Tristan? Is that you? No, it can't be you. You're lying on the ground, hurt.

In a cracked whisper: "I love you, Hess."

Gradually, I become aware of arms—warm arms—lifting me, of a greenish light shining just beyond the darkness of my closed eyelids. I imagine myself opening my eyes twice before I actually muster enough strength to open them for real.

All three times I see Tristan's face looking tenderly down at me.

"Tris!" I cry. "You're okay!"

I throw my wings around him, and he pulls me close. "I love you, too," I murmur. I'm so happy to see him—so relieved, so overcome—that I don't think about how tightly we hold each other. Or how his cheek touches mine, sending little tingles shooting all through me. Or how his lips brush past mine in something too gentle to be a kiss. . . .

Tristan is the first to pull away, his face filled with all the caution, and all the yearning, I feel. For a moment we stare at one another, each mirroring the turmoil in the other's eyes. And then, before I can think or hesitate or fear, we're holding each other again. Holding each other and slowly, ever so softly, kissing. Thrilling, ever so sweetly, soaring.

This time I'm the first to pull away, my heart thumping as fast as it would after a bounce-flight. This time, instead of looking at each other, we look down, as if we're both struck with an illogical interest in the plain dirt floor beneath us.

Well, you were right, Marcie. You were right.

Good old Marcie. I can just imagine her now, giggling with delight after I tell her that Tristan kissed me. "Yeah?" she'll say. "And then what? Then what happened?" (She won't mind, of course, because she'll already like someone else by the time I tell her.)

"Well," I'll say, "then we just kind of stared down at the floor."

"Yeah?" she'll squeal, her eyes bulging with excitement. "And then—let me guess! Then you pledged your undying love for each other and he asked you if you had a date for prom yet."

"Um, not exactly," I'll say. "You see, he's not really human. He's a Dyaphinee. They probably don't even bother having proms on his planet. I mean, no matter how dressed up they get, they can still see through each other, right down to their illumes."

Marcie will frown, bewildered. "Huh?"

"Oh, forget it, will you? To me he's an alien, and to him I'm an alien. It'll never work out. Not on the Alula plane, not on the human plane, not on the barren plane, definitely not on his planet! So stop bugging me about him."

"Hess."

It's Tristan's voice that interrupts my reverie. Tristan's face I look up to meet: probing, as always—but with a look so caring that it stings like the glare of the sun. "Are you okay?"

I touch the back of my head, remembering that it hurts there. "Well, my head aches a little, but. . . ." It's then that I notice his back legs—both of them, set in crude casts and tucked carefully beneath his horse's trunk.

"Broken," he answers my gasp. "The Alulas took good care of them, though. And they gave me something for the pain."

I quickly survey the room. Bare, dimly lit, stale-smelling. But most of all, closed-in: no chance of escape via the interplane. "We must be inside the High Skymount. They wouldn't keep us anywhere else but there."

From somewhere behind me, a small voice says: "You're right."

I turn sharply. There, framed by the little circle opening in the wall, is the face of a frightened, brown-eyed Alula.

"Nitza!" I cry, hastening to my feet.

"Shhh! I'm not supposed to be here."

"You're in trouble, aren't you? For letting me go." I walk to the wall. "Why . . . why did you, Nitza? Was it because you knew the voices came from the human plane?"

Her eyes long to answer me, but she stays silent.

"Is there any way out of here?" asks Tristan.

"No." She glances shyly at him, then looks back at me. "Not unless. . . ."

"Unless you let us out," I finish, my voice

grave.

Panic flashes across her face. Shaking her head: "No, I cannot! I'm not even supposed to be here."

"What are they planning to do with us?" asks Tristan.

She nervously checks behind her before answering. "They'll force Hesper to help them kill the . . . your kind."

"Force her? How?"

She looks from Tristan to me and back again. There's something familiar in her face —something that reminds me of the way I feel in school whenever I see couples kissing by the lockers. "How do you think?" she says, one eyebrow raised.

Tristan and I turn to each other. As our eyes meet, his tell me that he's sorry, that he's just as much at the mercy of his emotions for me. I think about how he held me, how it felt for our lips to touch, and a warm pleasure sweeps through me—a strange kind of pleasure that hurts. Quickly, I turn back to Nitza, hating the way Tristan and I feel about each other, not wanting at all for us to feel this way. But not wanting us *not* to, either.

Did Nitza see us kissing? I guess she did.

I guess I'll never be quite this embarrassed again as long as I live.

Though it's unnecessary now, Nitza explains to Tristan: "They know Hesper cares a lot about your life. They plan to use that."

"But they won't," I say, hopeful. "Not if you let us out, they won't!"

"Shhh!" She shakes her head, apologetic, clearly torn. "I cannot let you go, Hesper. The Council has the key. And they're already suspicious of me. If I let you out, I could never be a Council member. They would take away my privileges as a blood relative and Council-trainee. Treat me like any other young Alula."

"Send you," I say.

"Yes," she says quietly. "Send me." Her face gets smaller as she backs away from the opening. "I'm sorry, Hesper. I cannot let them Send me. I wouldn't know how to come back the way you do. I would be lost—forever lost—and I wouldn't even know it." She takes two more steps back, turns around.

"Nitza, wait!" I press my face against the rough edges of the hole in the wall. "Come with us then! We'll show you how to do it without forgetting. Just let us out."

"Hesper," I hear Tristan say from behind

me. His voice sounds wary.

When Nitza turns around again, her eyes are shiny with tears. "You—you trust me enough to share that secret?"

I look into her eyes. So scared. So unhappy. "I do," I say, nodding.

She considers it for a while. "You should not."

"What?"

"The Council thought you would trust me. That's why they made me come here. Why—before—they made me talk to you and let you go the way I did."

My stomach abruptly feels sick. "You mean . . . all of it . . . it was all planned?"

Her eyelids drop.

"You mean that everything you've just said . . . ?"

She turns back around, her head down and tilted slightly to the side. "I'm sorry I could not be a true friend to you, Hesper."

I gulp. "Nitza, wait. Nitza!"

I watch her long, dark hair fly out behind her as she runs, noiseless, down the tunnel-way.

22

Sky Bounce

Will they punish her? Will they Send her? I can't help but wonder as I stare out into the dim vacancy she left behind. Poor Nitza. She couldn't help us, but she couldn't hurt us either. I wonder. . . .

Tristan's voice interrupts my wondering. "Hess, we've got to find a way out of here. Fast."

The urgency in his voice is contagious. Again I can practically feel my missing hands start shaking. I walk over and flop down beside him. "I know, Tris. But how? Our only hope just ran down the tunnelway."

Silence.

"I mean, how else can we get out? The door's locked. The opening's too small to crawl through. What are we supposed to do— dig through the floor using my feet and your hands?"

He heaves a strained sigh, sifts his fingers

roughly through his hair, as if to stimulate his brain to think. Finally: "There's no other way but the interplane."

I roll my eyes. "Do you know where we are? We're sitting inside a room inside a sky-mount. Closed in by wall, soil, rock—"

"It's the only way, Hess. We've got to try it."

I stare at him in disbelief. From that all-too-familiar look on his face, I can tell he's switched into his let's-convince-Hesper-to-do-something-crazy mode. "Tristan! The inter-planar drift factor. We'll get stuck somewhere for sure!"

He nods solemnly. "Maybe, maybe not. We'll have to take that chance."

"I can't believe you!" I say. "The most elementary rule of interplanar travel, and you're ready to scrap it, just like that."

"Well, what other choice do we have? You just said yourself there's no way out. Sure, it's dangerous, but we need to get out of here. *Now*."

"But—"

"Either that or sit here and wait for the Council."

My right wing twitches. "Ohhhhhhhhh!" I

get up and pace around the room, longing for hands to wring. "If only we could have bounce-flown! We would have escaped!" I stop pacing and look down at his bright, up-lifted face. "Oh, Tris, I'd have given anything to bounce-fly again. Even my memory."

He turns away, draws little circles in the dirt with his finger. "You mean, just to bounce-fly, you would have been willing to forget me?"

"No—no, I didn't mean. . . ."

He stops drawing and says, half to me, half to the floor: "Because I wouldn't want to for-get you, Hess. Not ever. Not even to bounce-fly."

His words, and the sincere way he says them, fill my ears as briefly and beautifully as a song that ends before I can dance to it. I want to fly right after them—those words. I want to fly right out and leave my body be-hind, just like I did in that dream—the one where I went bounce-flying in my own back-yard. Bounce-flying by myself. Bounce-flying without wings or hooves or even a body. . . .

I gasp like someone just remembering to breathe. "Tris!" I exclaim. "You're right! We *do* have to ride the interplane. And we can!" I sit down across from him. "On the human plane, I dreamt that I bounce-flew with my illume. Only it wasn't a dream; it was real. And afterward I saw my body lying in my bed—*in*side my room, *in*side my house! My body had been there all the time, and it hadn't drifted."

My heart beats fast as I take Tristan's hands in my wings. Then his fingers close over my feathers, and my heart speeds up even more.

"Tris, there shouldn't *be* any interplanar drift factor. Not if we trust completely. Because if we put every last bit of trust in the Great Alula, how can any harm come to us? It's only if we let in that doubt, that fear, that our bodies can get stuck."

Tristan smiles an enlightened smile. "You know, you're right." Wonder is in his voice, but as he searches my face, his smile fades into worry. "It's still risky, though. If we panic, our bodies are in real danger of getting stuck."

The gravity of this warning closes in on me like the walls looming around us. We fall silent for a while, weighing it. Then all at once, we speak, Tristan's voice no less than a

syllable behind mine, sounding like a premature echo when we both ask:

"Are you afraid?"

I shake my head; he shakes his head: no. I
laugh, he laughs—laughs back at me like my
own reflection, chasing away all the tension.

"To the barren plane then?" he says, his
voice little more than a whisper.

"Yes."

He leans forward, and trembling, I do the
same. When I feel the warmth of his arms
wrapping around me, of his hands stroking the
same unkempt curls that always used to irk
him so, I know it could be for the last time. I
want him to kiss me—more than I'd like to
admit, I want him to—but when our lips do
meet, when we do wordlessly show how much
we cherish each other and all our alienness,
the ache inside me only gets stronger.

We part without wanting to, the sole reason our hurry to escape the Council. We don't
close our eyes until we've gazed one final
time at each other.

"Great Alula," Tristan quietly recites,
"God, Eternal One of many names . . ."

I take a deep breath and listen, trying to
focus on the words I hear instead of the anxi-

ety I suddenly feel. But I can't stop my stomach from tensing up or my head from pounding like a second heart.

". . . please take us safely to the plane of our choosing: the barren plane—a world parallel, at once here and not here . . ."

What if I can't trust enough? I think, though I'm not supposed to be thinking. *What'll happen to me? What if my body gets stuck and my illume leaves without it? I'll die for sure, crushed inside wall or rock.*

". . . please help us trust in you completely as you guide us to our destination. . . ."

Inside me, the doubt is like the sick sinking panic of falling without wings, without hope of bouncing. I close deeper my eyes. Tell myself to let go. Remind myself how it felt in the jelly dome, knowing I had an illume.

Knowing it. In a lightning-tingling.

Feeling it. In a sense-remembering.

Needing no other proof but the certainty within me. And believing, believing.

I feel Tristan's hand touch my wing, and unlike when we returned from the barren plane, I don't jump. It's as if he's discerned my battle and wants to soothe me. Without opening my eyes, I lean into him, and he slides his arm around me in a comforting half-embrace. Almost at the same time, I hear a voice—not one of the sad voices, but my mom's, repeating the Bible quote she said at the dinner table; and though she's on another plane and can't know what's going on, I can tell she's talking to me, reassuring me, just as surely as Tristan did the year we were apart.

"I sought the Lord, and He answered me; He delivered me from all my fears."

At last, feeling the love in Tristan's touch and the love in Mom's voice, and realizing that both come from God, I let the fear drop away—effortlessly, like baggage that's easier dumped than carried—and with a great inward sigh, I trust in God.

The vibration comes first, stronger than ever. Lifting me. Spreading me out into a space with no confinement—no limit to my shape, no weight of my body holding me back. Next comes a floating upward, through the ceiling, through the soil above, past rocks I could reach out to touch and not even feel. Yet there isn't time to reach out. For just as I want to, the High Skymount's surface drops behind and the sky rises ahead: wide, beckoning, drawing me up like a marionette strung on rays of morning sunshine. Up, up I fly—faster and higher than I ever could with wings—then down, down, I fall, straight for another sky-mount.

But you can't bounce-fly off a skymount, I think.

And then I bounce-fly off the skymount. Again and again I do it—down and up, down and up I soar in a wingless, hoofless sky bounce—until the pull snaps me into the familiar dark whir of the interplane, leaving nothing but the lightness inside, the peaceful lightness that is everything.

I wasn't afraid!

I want to shout it; I want to laugh it. But all I can do is let it quake through me in a joyous thunderclap quiet.

I wasn't afraid!

23

A New Danger

Stars. Colored stars, all clustered together.

That's what I think I see once the darkness of the interplane transforms into the darkness of the barren plane's sky. But I'm not looking from the ground up; I'm looking from the sky down. Way-up-high-in-the-sky down. And as I slowly float-fall—the green glow in the corner of my eye falling with me—I realize these colorful stars aren't stars at all. They're water-lights.

"Hess, are you there?" comes Tristan's fluid voice from beside me.

"Right over here!" I call back.

Despite how high we are, I can still make out the glimmer of the jelly dome below us. Many of the Dyaphinees are crowded outside it, and the rest are filing out—most likely to get a better view of us. Or of Tristan, I guess. I scan the ground beyond this dazzling group and notice a second cluster of lights: a fainter one, a good distance away from the jelly dome. A chill shimmies down me. Somehow I feel there is the place I must land.

"Hey, Hess, say something—really loud."

"Why?"

"So everyone will know you're up here. So everyone will know you have an illume."

"Tris—"

"You couldn't surrender like that—you couldn't defy the interplanar drift factor—unless you had an illume. So you can't be a void."

"Tris, they don't know that. They don't know we were trapped inside a skymount and still rode the interplane."

"But there must be some way we could prove to them. . . ."

"There isn't," I say, surprised at the confidence I hear in my own voice. "It's up to them to have faith." I focus again on the cluster of lights far beyond the jelly dome. "Anyway, being invisible could come in handy."

"What?"

I don't tell Tristan when I start floating away because I don't want him to come after me. It isn't that I *decide* to float away, really. It's just that I feel drawn toward the distant group of Dyaphinees, and I can't ignore this inner tugging.

As I get closer, I see that the water-lights are gathered in the form of a bright circle, with the yellow one as its dimmer center. I land right outside the circle. It's the smoothest, most soundless landing I've ever had, but I still miss hearing Tristan complain about my hair falling in his face.

". . . and Aeon is too full of useless compassion to know it," spouts the voice of the yellow water-light. I cautiously come closer, feeling a very strong dread. "But the Eternal One knows. He knows that when beings commit offense after offense against Him, when they're no longer anything but voids with no shape, no color, no piece of Him left within them, they do not deserve His compassion. They deserve His wrath."

I peer between two water-lights and nearly gasp at what I see. The blotches of the yellow's illume are darkening again, only this time new clouds are swirling into existence like mud stirring to the surface of a pond. Looking around at the other Dyaphinees' illumes, I notice the same thing happening to them, only to a lesser degree.

The yellow continues, "And what does the Eternal One do with voids so beyond hope that He grows sick at the sight of them—if even *He* can see these gaping holes that illumes should fill?" Pausing for a moment: "My friends, He destroys them."

I can't help but gasp now, though no one hears me over the murmur of Dyaphinees voicing their agreement. "Yes," they say. "It's true."

A purple water-light glides forward. "But Aeon will never allow it."

"Aeon," says the yellow, "will never suspect it. We'll simply go along with him. Apologize for challenging him in front of the . . . 'Alula.' Then when our chance comes, we'll carry out the Eternal One's true will by destroying these humans—these voids—that are too far gone to save."

I don't stay for any more; I rush as fast as I can to the jelly dome. It's a long way off, but I find that I reach it faster than I could with physical legs. And I'm not out of breath either. I sigh, relieved, at the sight of Tristan's illume and Aeon's, and all the others who crowd around and listen as I tell what I've witnessed.

"He said *I* was not the Eternal One," Aeon

says after I've finished. "Yet he claims for himself the Eternal One's power to judge and condemn." For the first time, I hear sorrow in Aeon's voice. "How could I have failed to foresee it? I knew it could affect us—to live among the humans. But I didn't realize how easily it would puff some of us up with pride." He falls silent for a moment, then continues, his words pushed along by an urgent current. "We must take them away from this planet. For in their judgment of others, they have tainted themselves to the point where they could indeed hasten the blending, just as the Alulas fear."

"But how can you make them leave?" I ask.

"Our whole group must leave," says Aeon. "They won't leave unless the whole group does."

Leave? I think. *Tristan, leave? So soon?*

I look in panic to the green illume beside me as Tristan voices the same distraught reaction: "All of us? Are you sure?"

"Yes," says Aeon. "We can trick them. We'll tell them that since the Alulas couldn't receive our message, we can't do anything but leave and let this planet self-destruct. Then, once we reach our planet, we'll have them detained while we return here to continue spreading our message." He pauses, and the next time he speaks, his voice flows once again with its usual joy. "Thank you, Hesper. You've helped us more than we ever hoped."

I look at him in surprise. "I failed, though. I couldn't make the Alulas understand."

"You've alerted us to this dangerous plot so that we can prevent it. And as for the Alulas, I did not ask you to make them understand. Only to tell them."

"Still, I'm sorry."

"Don't be." Aeon floats backwards a little. "And now Hesper, I must ask you to return to your life on the human plane."

"But, Aeon!" Tristan's cry echoes my own silent one.

"Tristan, where else do you think she can go?" Aeon says patiently. "She can't go back to her life as an Alula—not only because of what the Council would do, but because her awareness is higher now than a being of the Alula plane should be. Yet she surely can't come with us."

"Why not?" I ask, desperate. "I want to come with you. I want to see your planet!"

A ripple-smile runs down Tristan's illume like the sigh of a lake's surface under a strong breeze. "I never thought I'd hear you say something like that," he says. "You don't know how good it sounds."

Aeon's voice is sympathetic, yet firm. "I, too, am glad to hear you're brave enough to want to come, Hesper. But this is the very reason why you belong on the human plane now. For you've reached the rightful awareness of a being on the human plane. And you would best serve yourself and us if you returned there as one of our messengers."

"Me?" I ask, feeling very small. "But how could I? I wouldn't know what to do, what to say. . . ."

"You wouldn't have to do or say anything," Aeon explains. "You would just go on with your everyday life as a human girl. Only, some of those who came in contact with you—those who were ready and not too afraid—would start to feel the same truth you've felt."

"I see."

Aeon continues, "You won't be alone forever, Hesper. As soon as we can, we'll return to this planet to continue spreading our message this way—not by announcing it, but by living on the human plane and passing on to the humans the awareness they've lost. If you go there ahead of us now, you can start to quell the cries of the voices. Will you do this for us, Hesper?"

His voice fills me with its laughter, its joy. "Of course I will," I say. And with the laughter bubbling up into my own voice, I add, "After all, I do miss my mom and dad." But I also miss Tristan already, so despite the peaceful effect of Aeon's presence, I can't stop the sadness from coming. "I want to remember, though. I don't care if I have to be armless or legless or toothless. I need to remember!"

Aeon sighs a light water sigh. "It's not necessary to keep your memory to carry out your duty. It's your choice, but the interplane will take something, and it would be better to sacrifice your memory."

I stare into Aeon's dazzling blue, torn between what I know to be right and what my heart cannot bear. "I know," I whisper.

"Please don't worry, Hesper. Whether or not you sacrifice your memory, there's a part deep inside you that never forgets."

I turn to Tristan. I can't see his eyes looking back at me, but their essence I can see: the light that always reached up from behind. "I won't forget you, Tris." I want to say much more, but I feel uncomfortable with Aeon and the other Dyaphinees listening.

When Tristan answers, I can imagine him looking at me in his caring way. "Oh, Hess, this is the worst plane for good-byes. All I have is your voice."

I come closer to his water-light form— close enough to smell the moisture of the water, to feel the warmth of the light. "If I never bounce-fly again," I say, "that's fine with me. But if I never see you again. . . ." The emotion in my voice finishes my sentence for me.

Tristan's voice, too, is full of feeling. But his words are tinged with a familiar hope. "I didn't find you just to lose you again, Hess. We *will* see each other. Soon. Not on this plane, but another."

"Yes: another," I say. Cheerfully, for Tristan's sake.

24

That Which Never Forgets

The first thing I do after I reach school and stop at my locker is look for the boy in the wheelchair. I look everywhere—even in that awful courtyard—but I still can't find him.

Where is he? I wonder. *Is he sick? Skipping? Where has he gone?*

I'm about to head back outside to check the deserted field when, unfortunately, Marcie finds me.

"Hesper, wait up!"

I'm practically out the door when I hear her call, but I turn and wait for her anyway.

"Hey, cool haircut!" she says.

"The only thing cool about it is my neck." I run my fingers through my now-above-shoulder-length curls. I feel so disoriented that I can't even recall getting my hair cut. "I feel like I've lost a limb or something."

"Oh, Hesper, don't exaggerate. Hey, do you believe in love at first sight?"

"Huh?"

"Well," she breathes, a smile flushing her face pink, "I only got a glimpse of him, but I think I'm in love! And from the way he looked at me, I think he just might be, too! You've gotta help me think of a way to meet him. He's tall, and he's got blond hair, blue eyes, the most awesome smile—"

"Marcie, have you seen the boy in the wheelchair?"

She frowns. "Who? Oh! No, I haven't. I think he moved or something. But you know, maybe he isn't right for you after all. I mean, he is cute, but you're not into hang gliding—"

"I'm sorry, but I've got to go somewhere now," I cut in as nicely as I can. "I'll talk to you in third period. You can tell me all about your new guy then, okay?"

"Oh, okay," I hear her grumble as I turn to walk out the door.

I turn so fast that I nearly bump right into a girl on her way inside. We both step back and, for a few seconds, stand there on either side of the doorway. She's a serious-looking girl with wide brown eyes that stare at me in a very striking way before she catches herself and shyly looks down. For some reason, I'm filled with an overwhelming sympathy for her—this girl I don't know, can't know, yet somehow feel that I should know, *do* know. Just like I knew the boy in the wheelchair.

I hesitate before moving to the side.

She smiles, and I notice her front teeth are a little crooked. "Thanks," she mumbles.

As she passes, I get an urge to comfort her, but I have no idea why.

"Hey, wait," I say—I'm compelled to say —from behind her.

She turns slowly, uncertainly.

I ask, "Um . . . do you have algebra with Mr. Cole?"

"Yeah," she says, still shy.

I smile. "Me, too. Do you understand the chapter we're on now?"

"Yeah."

"Well, do you think you could explain it to me. During lunch, maybe?"

It's a strange favor to ask of someone who doesn't even know you, and I have no idea why I say it. But to my relief, she looks back at me almost gratefully, as if I've offered her my help instead of asking for hers. "Okay, at lunch," she says. "Meet me outside the cafeteria."

We're meant to be friends, I think as I continue out the door and on to the deserted field.
*Why is it I know she and I are meant to be
friends?*

I hurry across the street, stepping over an
old newspaper on the way. The headline
flashes by, but the words stick: "Student Ser-
vice Club Helps Community." I decide to pick
up the paper on my way back, and for the first
time in a long while, I find myself wanting to
watch the news tonight.

Soon I reach the spot where yesterday
morning I set down my books, purse, and
comb. They're all there, just as I left them—
though I thought I *hadn't* left them. I sit on the
ground to study my comb's smashed remains,
replaying everything over again in my mind.
The boy in the wheelchair talked me into trav-
eling to his plane. I tried it, and when I closed
my eyes, I lost my balance, I stomped on my
comb, and nothing happened. So I went to
class.

But did I *really?* How could I have been
so absentminded as to go to class and leave all
my stuff in the field?

A large flock of birds alights on the telephone wire by the road. I watch the wire, thick

with so many birds. I stare back down at the remains of my wooden comb, and as I do, I get the most extraordinary feeling, like I've misplaced a piece of myself. Like something in me broke off the same way my comb's teeth broke off.

"What's wrong with me?" I say aloud. To the field, the comb, the still flock of birds. "Did something happen? Or am I going crazy?"

With a rustle, the birds fly out in a long fluid mass that ripples down and up again like one giant wing flapping. And the answer comes then: in a tremble, a great lightness arising from deep within me. And in the sound of a faraway voice, whispering a tender farewell, and making me remember.

About the Author

Deanna Miller has worked as a cashier, ESL tutor, technical writer, nanny, copy editor, and journal managing editor. She currently copy-edits for a weekly newsmagazine. In addition to book writing, her interests are songwriting, singing, dancing, and human rights activism.

Also by Deanna Miller:

Time to Tell 'Em Off!
A Pocket Guide to Overcoming
Peer Ridicule

"A highly recommended social survival guide for young people everywhere and should be included in every school and community library collection in the country."
—*The Children's Bookwatch*

"Encourages readers not to make the mistake of believing what bullies want them to believe—that there's something wrong with them."
—*Canadian Living* magazine

"Helps teens take a look at themselves and learn to like what they see, instead of hearing and believing hurtful words from others."
—Penny Morang Richards, *Eagle-Tribune*

"Definitely ideal for those currently bearing the burden of being teased."
—*Swerve Magazine* editors, http://jump.to/swerve

Read a free excerpt on the Web:
http://www.deannamiller.com/excerpts.html